One for the Money

Skye Warren

CHAPTER ONE

Eva

BLACK TUXEDOS. GLITTERING gowns. Splashing champagne.

These things are common in my life. Mundane. I grew up under the warm glow of chandeliers. Laughter and conversation were my lullabies, the sound drifting up the spiral staircase to our bedrooms. I learned the planning of these events from my mother, the same way other daughters learn to quilt or bake or garden.

This particular gala benefits the Society for the Preservation of Orchids.

Ironic, considering the number of orchids we had to kill to build the elaborate sculpture in the foyer. My mother sits on the board. She doesn't care about flowers.

She cares about connections.

It's the family business, really. Making deals in ballrooms.

My father waves me over to him. He's officially retired. Stepped down as CEO of Morelli Holdings. Replaced by my brother Lucian. Unofficially, he'll only stop working when he's six feet underground. It's just the way he was made.

"Hi, Dad." I give him a dutiful kiss on his cheek.

He pulls me close to his side. His mood is magnanimous. Probably because there's a congressman, a famous filmmaker, and an oil tycoon from Texas hanging on his every word. "This is my daughter, Eva. Have you met her? She's the one responsible for all this."

The group responds with enthusiastic praise.

"The arbor is absolutely inspired," the filmmaker says. "The way you used crepe paper to mimic the tree bark, the way the branches wind above you. It feels like you're walking through a real forest. If you ever want to do set design, you have a place in L.A."

My father's hand tightens on my arm. "We could never let her go."

I manage a gracious smile. "High praise, indeed. But you're right. I could never leave New York. It's home."

The oil tycoon winks. "That's right. I tried to lure her down to Texas. Unlimited barbecue and a swimming pool as big as a basketball court couldn't sway her."

My cheeks flush with old embarrassment. The man is handsome enough, in a white-haired kind of way. Smart enough. And definitely rich enough. But he didn't even bother asking me out. No, he went straight to my father and offered to buy me in a business deal.

As if I were a head of cattle.

I excuse myself and stride away, directing a server to refill their glasses. I know what each of them likes to drink. I know where their vacation homes are and what racehorses they own. It's part of my role as hostess, to make everyone comfortable.

To make everyone comfortable except for me.

My face feels tight from smiling. My feet ache from running around all day. I wore flats until the gala started, then I switched into heels, but it didn't help. My calves are burning.

Since things are smooth in the ballroom, I swing through the kitchen. One of the cooks is shouting obscenities at a server who dropped a plate of appetizers. Even I have to cringe at the loss. Each large white spoon contains a thin slice of Japanese Shorthorn Wagyu beef with caviar and mascarpone cream, topped with delicately sliced jalepeños, red onion, and Asian pear.

"Clean this up," I say to the server, mostly to get him away from the cook. Will he hire him again? Maybe not, but there's no point making him cry in the middle of service. Then I address the cook. "Do we have any more of that caviar?"

"Yes," he growls, still frustrated. "None of the beef."

"Serve it on crostini with crème fraîche."

"I don't serve boring food."

"You do unless you want the people to go home hungry."

He curses fluently but turns to prepare the tray. My work here is done. For now, anyway. I head back upstairs. On the way I pass the head bartender, who looks harried.

"We're out of champagne," he says, panic in his voice.

"How is that possible?"

The top of his bald head shines with sweat. He used to be a top sommelier at a five-star hotel, but a few hundred of Bishop's Landing's elite reduces him to a nervous breakdown. "Some young men. They wanted the bottles for beer pong. Champagne pong, they called it."

"And you gave it to them?"

"Of course not." He looks indignant. Then he sighs. "Mrs. Crockett asked after that vintage of Chardonnay she likes, and I went down to the wine cellar to get it. Then when I got back, two entire cases of champagne were gone."

I press two fingers to the middle of my forehead. No champagne. If we aren't careful, we'll have a full-scale revolt on our hands. "We have white wine, right?"

"Plenty, madam."

"The signature cocktail of the night is now a white wine spritzer, designed to celebrate both the simplicity and the depth of orchids. Have the bartenders offer it first. If we're giving them something delicious and sparkling, they should be content."

"And if someone requests champagne specifically?"

"There's a couple bottles of Armand de Brignac in my father's study." Which I'll have to replace before he notices it's gone. He won't appreciate having his private stash picked over. Then again, he wouldn't like to have the guests denied.

That crisis averted, I continue working my way through the room.

My mother waves me over. "There's someone I want you to meet," she says, and she's already smiling. Which means he must be nearby. And powerful.

"Who?" I know the entire guest list for this event, which means I know everyone in the room. Maybe not personally, but I know their names and their net worth. Those are the main things that matter in high-society circles.

An older man waits near the balcony door. He wears the black tuxedo well. He clearly works out. And if his hairline is receding, well, he can hardly help that. He looks to be in his forties, maybe ten years older than me. I recognize him as being in the manufacturing industry. "You must be Mr. Langley," I say.

"I see my reputation precedes me," he says, laughing. "Call me Alex."

"How long are you staying in New York?" I ask, being polite. He's got factories throughout the flyover states, but his home is in Chicago if I remember correctly.

"For a long time, perhaps. I'm thinking of moving to the East Coast."

"Are you?" I say, my stomach sinking as I realize why my mother wanted to introduce us. It's her attempt at matchmaking. The irony is that if I actually got married and started my own family, my mother would probably have a nervous breakdown. My father would get arrested for being drunk and disorderly. And my siblings would need something from me. Having money smooths a lot of life's hard edges, but it doesn't blunt them completely. We still need someone to handle the details. To get my mother her Xanax, to call the lawyer. To de-escalate every situation. We need a manager. And in the Morelli family, ever since I turned fifteen, that's been me.

He gives me a vaguely paternal smile. "It's time for me to start a family."

Not exactly subtle, Alex. "I wish you luck, then."

"Eva planned this little gala," my mother says, breezing past my comment. "She creates the most memorable displays. People talk about them for months."

"The perfect hostess," he says, clearly approving.

Bile rises in my throat. Now I know what a racehorse feels like when it's being checked over. *Good teeth. A friendly disposition. Will look nice pulling your carriage.*

"Speaking of hosting, I should check back in the kitchens."

I make a break for it, but my mother catches up with me. She leads me into an empty hallway and a darkened drawing room.

"Sit with me," she says. "I feel like we've been circling all night. I haven't had a chance to really see you."

"I'm right here."

We *have* been circling all night. That's what we always do, me managing one side of the room while she manages the other. We even do it at family dinners, her with my father, me handling my brothers. We spend untold energy keeping the peace in the Morelli household.

She hands me a glass filled with spritzer.

"It's very good," she says.

She usually doesn't leave this long in the middle of a gala. "Can I get you anything?"

"Langley is worth a nice seven billion."

"Mother."

She adopts an innocent expression. "Do you *want* to marry someone poor?"

"I don't want to marry anyone. And definitely not Alex Langley."

"His wife died five years ago. He's been mourning her. Sweet, don't you think?"

"Then why are you trying to set us up?"

"If you must know, he asked after you. He's

ready to start a family. He wants someone mature, closer in age to him than the debutantes, but still beautiful. You fit the bill."

"How flattering."

All of us wear masks. My mother is the exquisite beauty and perfect hostess. She lets the mask slip only rarely. I've only met the true Sarah Morelli a handful of times.

This is one of those times.

Her green eyes are an endless field. "Not flattering, Eva. No. Don't look to men for flattery. Not if you want to be someone's wife. Flattery is for their girlfriends. Their mistresses. Their whores. Not the women by their sides."

"Why would I want to be someone's wife?"

"Security. Connections. Children. The same reasons women have gotten married for hundreds of years. Thousands of years, probably. Humans haven't evolved that far."

"Then it won't matter much if the evolutionary line ends with me."

The wall goes back up. In the blink of an eye I'm looking at the serene expression of a society hostess, as remote and poised as anyone. Not my mother. "You'll want children eventually. All women do. Don't wait too long."

I've heard that line before. There are arguments I could make. *Not all women want to be mothers. And that's fine. Feminism is about letting women choose their own path.*

The words stick in my throat.

Not all women want to be mothers, but in my secret heart, I do.

"Is now really the time?" I ask, my words tight.

"You have to settle down at some point."

"Why?"

"So you have your own home."

"I'm not homeless, Mom."

"A real home, not a loft filled with knick-knacks. A husband can give you that."

"This is the twenty-first century. And in case you haven't noticed, I'm loaded. I could buy a house if I wanted. I already own houses, actually."

"Places," she says. "Buildings. Not homes."

"Because it doesn't have a penis in it?"

Her eyelids flutter closed. "Eva Honorata Morelli."

I look past her toward the large picture window. "The truth is that I would like children, but I'm not willing to live in a loveless marriage for that."

It's beautiful out there. Green and maintained and lush. Beautiful the way the inside of the house is beautiful. Grand and a little intimidating. It's the kind of house I would preside over if I made a society marriage to someone like Langley.

Her tone is conciliatory. "There's security for a woman in marriage."

"And give up my freedom?"

"My relationship with your father is complicated. It doesn't have to be that way for you. The man I just introduced you to is a good man. You can trust him."

"I can't trust anyone," I say flatly. Because I can't. Security? Acceptance in society? That's not what you get when you go with a man. That's not what you bet on. Ever.

My mother studies me, looking bemused. We're close as far as mothers and daughters go, but I've never told her why I don't trust men. And I won't be telling her tonight.

The door to the sitting room opens.

A man stands there in a tux that speaks of wealth and a bearing that says his family has had it for generations. Privilege. Power. And enough self-awareness to make it feel like an inside joke that you're part of. Phineas Hughes was a few years behind me when I came up in society. We've met. And everyone knows about them. The Hughes family is like the Kennedys or the

Vanderbilts—steeped in luxury. Though we've never spoken for very long.

Blonde hair gleams beneath the low lighting.

Hazel eyes twinkle with roguish charm.

"Finn Hughes," my mother exclaims, her cheeks pinkening, her eyes going bright.

She lifts her glass just a little, and I wish I had a Diet Coke instead of the spritzer. I feel my own cheeks heating, but I don't flutter my eyelashes like my mother does. I don't act surprised to see him, even though I have no idea what he's doing here.

"Mrs. Morelli," Finn says with a playful bow. He doesn't need to be handsome or well-built. Not when he's the oldest son of one of the most powerful families in the country. He's painfully rich, but that doesn't stop him from also being charming. It's honestly annoying.

"I told you to call me Sarah," my mother scolds, flirting with a man half her age.

"Mrs. Morelli," he says, refusing her with so much grace and respect that she can't be offended. "It's always a pleasure to see you again. I came looking for your daughter."

Excitement rushes through me like champagne, like caffeine. Me?

"Sophia's not here," my mother says.

She assumes a playboy like Finn Hughes, a man who could have whoever he wants, would want Sophia. She's the wild child. The one who could have adventures with him. And suddenly I feel old at the ripe old age of thirty-three. I don't go to exclusive night clubs. I don't get into trouble, if I can help it.

Instead I help my mother plan her events and help my siblings manage their lives. I help and help and help, and it never seemed quite so depressing until this moment.

My stomach sinks.

"I want Eva," he says, glancing at me. That devilish glint in his eyes promises mischief. And maybe even danger. It promises something entirely different than *help*. "We have plans."

He's lying, of course.

Though I don't know why.

Maybe he just wants to save me from this awkward conversation. Or maybe he really does need help—perhaps the lack of champagne has finally created chaos.

Sophia would be right for Finn. That's assuming he's ever looking to settle down, which I doubt. Wealthy. Handsome. And far too charming. Why would such a man choose marriage? My mother was right about one thing.

Marriage does have more benefits for the woman.

Men can do whatever they want.

Women like me? We have a ticking clock. There's only so long that I'll stay attractive to men like Langley. Only so long that I can have children. My heart squeezes thinking of all the years I've spent being helpful. Thinking of all the years I've spent trying to make sure that my family had what they needed. Paying attention to everything and everyone. Except myself.

And now it might be too late.

CHAPTER TWO

Finn

WE DON'T HAVE plans.

I made that up three minutes ago when I walked by and heard Sarah Morelli trying to set up her daughter with that older man from the gathering. I couldn't leave her there alone.

Alex fucking Langley for Eva? He's ancient.

Maybe not that much older than her, not so much older that it would be a scandal, but he's old. And boring. He's searching for a mate the way you find a mare for a stallion. For well-bred children. That's what these men want, a woman to bring them a drink at the end of the day, to be the hostess at events like this one. Plan everything, so he never has to think about anything. Do everything, so he only has to glad-hand at galas.

I'm going to get her out of here.

Surprise flashes through Sarah Morelli's eyes.

I know what I look like to her. A catch. She's put me next to Lizzy at past dinner parties, as if I might be interested in a child. We might be in the twenty-first century, but matches are still made. Arranged marriages happen every day in families like ours.

No, thank you.

I won't be getting married. Ever.

And I'm not particularly interested in the Morellis. Except for Eva. There's something about her that calls to me. The sense of innate sadness. It makes me want to cheer her up, which is something I can do—at least in a temporary way.

That's what I'm good for. Temporary.

"You didn't tell me you had plans," Sarah tells Eva, half scolding. The delighted smile on her face gives her away. It may surprise her, but she's nothing if not adaptable. Bagging a Hughes with any daughter would be a coup. "Where are you going?"

"Yes, Finn. Where are we going?" Eva asks, laughter in her voice.

I like this mischievous Eva better than the beleaguered one. Her dark eyes sparkle with silent challenge. It makes me hard beneath the thin wool of my tux. "It's a surprise."

"Indeed," Sarah murmurs, glancing between the two of us.

Suspicious? Perhaps, but she's not going to say no to me. Not because I'm persuasive or charming. She won't say no because my family is one of the most wealthy and powerful in the country. I could be a bastard, and Sarah would still hand me her daughter on a silver platter.

Eva's wine-red lips quirk in a half-smile. "As much fun as surprises can be, I think I should stay here. After the champagne drought, who knows what might go wrong?"

"We ran out of champagne?" Sarah glances at her almost-empty champagne glass. "Is that why we have a white wine spritzer as the signature cocktail? It's delicious, but I don't remember seeing it in the event plan."

It's time to issue my own subtle challenge to Eva Morelli. Enough of the event planning and the matchmaking. I'm strangled for air, and I've only been here a few minutes.

It's like she's being buried alive with piles of money.

"I can't tell you where we're going," I admit. "But I can tell you what we'll be doing. We're going to have a good time. Fun. You remember how to do that, don't you?"

A delicate snort.

"So much fun you'll lose track of time."

"Promises, promises."

"I don't make promises I don't keep," I tell her, looking into her dark, fathomless eyes. There's not much I can offer this woman, but I can offer her this.

Eva's expression flickers with wariness. And with curiosity.

Her mother looks scandalized by Eva's reaction to me. In another second, she'll open her mouth and demand that her daughter come with me. But I don't want Eva to come because her mother demands it. I want her to come because she chooses curiosity.

No, I want her to come because she chooses me.

I lean against the doorframe as if I have all the time in the world. Really, the opposite is true. "How about a bet? If you have a good time tonight, then I win. But if you, in your honest assessment, don't have a good time, you win."

"I'll win what, exactly?"

I reach into my pockets. A billfold. An old pocket watch. A handful of coins.

The quarter flips off my thumb and across the room. I didn't give her enough warning, but she captures it anyway. Delicate fingers smooth across the warm metal. "Twenty-five cents? I suppose I could add foam to my Starbucks order tomorrow."

"Have a wonderful meal," Sarah Morelli says.

Eva kisses her mother's cheek.

When she approaches me, her chin is high and her bearing regal, but there's a hint of vulnerability in her eyes. It's what pulls me to her. She's so damn strong, holding up her entire family like Atlas holds the world. But who rubs her shoulders at the end of the day?

I offer her my arm, and she takes it. Very formal.

There's nothing untoward about us. My body doesn't give a fuck. It reacts with a violent sense of victory. *Mine,* it says. The way her arm rests in mine, the heat of her body—it's like she was made to stand at my side.

Or maybe I was made to stand by hers.

Which is all just my body's way of telling me I'm down to fuck.

I don't think that's in the cards for me tonight, but I find I don't mind that much. The challenge is more appealing. The challenge to make Eva Morelli have fun. I escort her out of the room. We're all the way down the hall when she starts second-guessing herself. I feel it enter her limbs like stiffness. Like fear, even if she'd never admit it.

"We don't actually have to go anywhere," she murmurs, as if she's letting me off the hook. As if I should be relieved that I don't get to take her on a date.

"Chickening out already?" I ask.

Her glance is sharp. "Excuse me?"

"That's what this is, right? You're afraid I might actually make good on my promise. That you'd actually have a good time, while your family has to fend for themselves."

Rose blooms on her cheeks. A deep breath draws my attention to the shadowed space between her breasts. Indignation looks sexy on her. "Unlike my mother, I know that there weren't any real plans. You only said that to shock her. This is a game for you."

"A game?"

"A game," she says, "like everything else in your life. You have money and women and cars, and not a single problem that can't be solved by a check."

Anger blisters through my veins. Followed by grief. "If you say so."

"My mother's going to expect me to come up

with fantastical tales of this surprise date I somehow managed to land with the charming and handsome Finn Hughes."

"You think I'm handsome?"

An exasperated laugh. "She thinks you're handsome. I think you're annoying."

"You think I'm charming, for sure."

"And full of yourself."

I grin. "Come on, Morelli. Have a good time. I double-dog dare you."

She throws up her hands in the middle of the large, darkened hallway. "I can't even imagine leaving in the middle of a gala. What if something goes wrong?"

"Let it burn. We've got plans."

She shakes her head, a half-smile on her face. It's not refusal. It's the look of a woman who's going to let me show her a good time. I take her hand and lead her away from the bright lights. We leave through a side exit. Gargoyles watch us from the crown of the house as we go down. My Bugatti is already waiting there. I texted the valet before I even entered the drawing room. She's already purring in the gravel drive.

"Your car is already waiting?" Eva says, a laugh in her voice.

"What? I don't do half-assed promises. I stole

you away for the night. You're mine for the next five hours. What will I do with you? I have ideas, of course. Hundreds of them." I sweep open the door and hold it for her.

Eva hesitates for a heartbeat. Then she lets me hand her into the deep seat.

"Where are we really going?" she says. "Somewhere in the city?"

"No, somewhere here."

"Here as in Bishop's Landing?" she says. Because, of course, Eva grew up here.

She should know the places a person would go to have fun in Bishop's Landing. And I don't mean champagne fun, I mean alcohol fun. I mean blackout-and-forget fun. Or at least the possibility of it. The possibility of bliss.

"Yes," I tell her.

"Will you take me home afterward?"

"Back to your parents' house?" I ask.

"I don't live in the Morelli mansion," she says.

No, of course she doesn't. She lives in the city, but you wouldn't know it by how often she's here. Eva is always at her mother's society events.

She's always everywhere her family is.

"I'll take you home," I promise, knowing, even as I say it, that I'm never going to be able to drop her off at some ritzy loft in the city and drive away. I'll be thinking of her straight through the next year, and maybe even after that. I'll keep thinking and thinking and thinking until the thoughts turn into something filthy and rough, because I felt her body against mine.

It's a short drive to the small downtown of Bishop's Landing. I hook a right at an Italian restaurant that serves thin-crust pizzas as big as their tables. I keep driving down the alley. Cars gleam in a neat row behind closed businesses. Only one door has sound behind it.

During the day it's an art gallery. Right now it's something else entirely.

"Where are we?" she asks, whispering.

"The gallery. Don't you recognize it?"

"Are we going to steal a painting?"

"No, but I like the way you think. We can do that another night." I make a *tsk*ing sound when she tries to object. "But never fear. What we're about to do is also illegal."

Her eyes go wide in the dark. "*Finn.*"

I like her saying my name in that urgent, breathy way.

My body hardens. I'm having explicit ideas of ways I can take Eva in this alley. She'd probably like them, too. I've learned that high-society women enjoy a bit of roughness. They want something that silk sheets and bubble baths can't give them.

I knock on the door three times.

In the faint moonlight, Eva gazes up at me. She looks exhilarated, fully alive, and breathtakingly beautiful. It makes me want to corrupt her in every way I can imagine.

CHAPTER THREE

Eva

I'VE BEEN TO countless showings at this art gallery.

Apparently they deal in more than sculpture.

Clay pieces move across baize-covered tables. Alcohol flows freely. The underground poker club is in full swing when we arrive.

"How come I never knew about this place?"

"Overprotective brothers," Finn says with a shrug.

"Leo knows about this?" I ask, but then of course he does.

He knows everything that happens in Bishop's Landing and most things that happen in New York City. It would have been just like him to come here in his wild youth—and not tell me. His best friend. We're close, even for siblings.

But I can't quite shake the protectiveness out of him. "I'm going to kill him."

A fight breaks out over a table. Playing cards fly. Men in suits break it up.

It's over in a flash, but I find myself behind Finn. Somehow, in those few seconds, he put himself between me and danger. A shiver runs through me. A delicious one. That fistfight was a reminder that this *is* illegal. But playboy or not, Finn Hughes will protect me.

For this night only, he's mine.

"You okay?" he murmurs, his gaze assessing me, seeing if I'm freaked out by the fight. *Chickening out already?* he asked before we left. I'm determined to prove him wrong.

I make a show of looking at a nonexistent watch. "I'm okay, but it looks like you're on your way to losing twenty-five cold, hard cents in that bet."

"You don't stand a chance, sweetheart."

He leads me down a narrow staircase into an even darker room, with fewer tables and a singer wearing a sparkling dress. The high roller room. Of course a Hughes would be allowed into any room, but it's interesting to me that they don't even ask.

They know him by sight.

Glasses clink. Chips clack. Low laughter rolls beneath it all.

Finn puts down a small stack of hundreds.

It's immediately replaced by chips.

He puts the entire stack in front of me.

I feel my eyes go wide. "This is too much."

"I know what you're worth, Morelli."

It's not that I'm a frugal person. I was raised in luxury, and I like nice things. Money doesn't impress me. That's what comes from being raised an heiress.

I wouldn't blink an eye at an expensive dinner or some other purchase.

"Listen, I understand trading money for things. But I don't understand gambling. It's trading money for… what? Risk? The chance to lose everything?"

"For fun, sweetheart. Don't you ever pay for fun?"

A snort is not quite a ladylike answer. But it's true. Even the money I spend on behalf of my family doesn't feel recreational. No, it's about society. Status. And business.

I run my fingertip along the stack of clay chips.

It's a lot of money to spend on fun. And maybe I don't feel like I deserve it.

The dealer calls for the ante, and I push forward five hundred-dollar markers. That's the entry amount. The minimum to play the game.

It makes my heart pound.

Or maybe it's Finn, standing so close to my stool.

He's only standing so close because the rest of the stools are full, I'm sure. He's only leaning near me so he can see the cards on the table. If my heart beats faster, that's only because it's been so long since I've had a man's warm breath brush my temple. Since I've felt a man against my back, almost intimate despite the public setting.

Cards are dealt.

I don't play at casinos, underground or otherwise, but I know the basics. The pairs and the straights and the flushes. Which is how I know the cards in my hand are a whole lot of nothing. Suddenly that five-hundred-dollar ante feels like a fortune. It feels like a loss.

Why did I think this would be a good idea?

Disappointment sinks in my gut.

Then a low voice murmurs in my ear. "Patience. Good things come to those who wait."

My breath catches at the masculine purr. It feels like sex surrounding me, sensual cashmere that makes my eyes close. "I've been waiting a long time."

I'm not sure where the words come from. I didn't feel like I was waiting. I'm not Aurora sleeping in a forest, dreaming of a kiss from Prince Charming.

I have no interest in kisses.

And Finn Hughes is no Prince Charming.

He puts his hand on my hip. His thumb brushes my skin through the silk of my dress, back and forth, back and forth. It's startling. Intimate. It could be excused as a casual gesture between friends. The natural result of close proximity. Almost.

Except that it's faintly possessive.

I don't feel like a possession to be bought and sold. I don't even feel like a head of cattle to be bargained for. No, I feel like a jewel. Something to be coveted.

Something to hold close so that no one else steals it.

He caresses me through the bids, through the flop and the turn cards. I'm left with a single pair of eights. Not exactly auspicious, but better than nothing.

The dealer waits for the round of bidding before the river.

This is the last card, the one that determines

my hand for good.

So far none of the other players seem like they have incredible cards, but maybe they're hiding it well. Then again, two of the men seem enamored with the women who surround them. Three women for two men. And while the men wear suits, the women wear barely-there dresses that are more like glittering swimsuits. Not that I'm judging.

It just makes me feel old in my Dior ballgown.

It's not the ballgown. No, it's my actual age that makes me feel old.

Thirty-three is ancient for an unmarried woman in our social set.

We're waiting for the couple beside us to place their bet. They have to confer over every decision, using the opportunity to feel each other up.

They look deeply in love. Or deeply in lust. I'm not sure I even know the difference.

I glance back at the man who watches me.

His hazel eyes deepen to emerald as he looks back. "Go all in."

A startled laugh escapes me, but with our faces this close, my amusement dries up. It's replaced with whatever that couple has—not love, then.

Lust. I feel my body become liquid and heavy, as if I'm readying myself. I'm in a room full of people, but my body doesn't care about that. It wants to take this man. "You're insane."

"I'm interesting," he counters, his lip curling up.

"You're reckless."

"I'm interested," he says, and I know what he means. His tone makes it clear. His gaze does, too. He's interested in me, the same way the man is interested in the woman he's practically fingering on the stool next to us.

The dealer clears his throat so that they'll make their bid.

"You're young," I tell him, because it's the reason we can't be together. Not the real reason, but one that's socially acceptable. I'm not some aging widow who has a fling with the pool boy. Men his age don't hook up with women my age.

"Bullshit," he says.

"How old are you?"

"Twenty-nine."

I scoff. "Young."

His smile turns a little sad. "Age isn't about how long you've lived."

"That's *exactly* what it's about."

"It's about experience." He leans close, so he

can whisper. His lips brush the outer shell of my ear as he speaks, raising sparks of interest throughout my body. "And I think I have lots more experience than you. Don't worry, though. I'll break you in slowly."

"Break me *in*," I say, my voice too high. "Like I'm a horse."

"Don't be offended. My horses are thoroughbreds."

I know from society talk that Hughes racehorses are legendary. But I didn't know how much of that legacy trickled down to Finn. Enough, apparently. "I'm not a thoroughbred."

"Ma'am," the dealer says, snagging my attention.

The couple made their decision. They're in.

It's my turn. Two pair probably isn't enough to win this. But I'm only one diamond away from a flush. On the off chance I get it, that could be enough to win.

Or it might not be.

I don't like the uncertainty. It makes me nervous. Anxious.

Or maybe that's the way Finn watches me. As if he wants to prove a point. That I'm staid, dependable Eva Morelli. That I wouldn't know how to have fun if it kidnapped me and took me to an underground casino.

I push the piles of chips into the center.

A gasp sounds from the people around the table.

"Fuck," Finn murmurs, his hand tightening on my hip. "That was so hot."

The couple groans in unison and throws their cards down, quitting outside of their turn. The dealer brings the bet around again. Against my high raise, only one man remains. An elderly gentleman who looks severe with a poker face.

He looks, in Finn's words, experienced. I don't think he'd stay in with a poor hand.

Every muscle in my body clenches as I watch the dealer's hand.

He flips a card.

I blink, sure that I'm imagining it. An eight of diamonds sits on the green fabric. Holy shit. I got the flush that I was hoping for, but even more than that, I got a full house.

My fist shoots in the air. "*Yes.*"

Immediately my cheeks heat at the unladylike action.

Finn releases a low chuckle.

We're hardly being subtle, but it doesn't matter. There are already several thousand dollars in the pot. The older gentleman reveals a straight with a rueful smile.

"Congratulations," he tells me in a gruff voice.

Excitement overtakes my good sense and my dignity. I throw my arms around Finn's neck, laughing. His eyes sparkle blue and green hues. "I told you good things would come to those who wait," he says, his voice low and private. They aren't suggestive words, not really. But I feel the erotic suggestion throughout my body, at the tips of my breasts and between my legs. As if he's rewarding me after a long, tantric session.

"I'm thirty-three," I tell him, waiting for his shock, his stiffness.

Dreading the way he'll have to force a smile.

He searches my eyes. "Do you think that matters to me?"

"You're a playboy. A rascal. You can have your pick of any woman inside this casino. And any woman outside of it. Why would you want me?"

"A rascal," he says, laughing. "Who says rascal anymore?"

Despite my embarrassment, despite my awkwardness, I find myself laughing with him. Laughing so hard tears prick my eyes. "See? I told you. I'm an old grandma."

He shakes with silent humor before becoming

serious again. "Eva. You're an incredibly sexy woman. A bombshell. A goddamn dream. Any man would want you, me included."

I stop breathing for a ten count. "You do?"

"Men must make passes at you all the time. Women, too."

A knot forms in my throat.

"But you don't believe them," he guesses. "You think they're after your money."

I force a shrug. "It's not unlikely. You know what I'm worth. So do other people. They want my money or even just my connections to my family. But that's not why I don't pay attention when someone makes a pass at me."

"Then why?"

"Because I'm over love." The words come out fast and honest. It scares me, how much I liked the excitement. Winning. How much I wanted to do it again. How much I enjoy having Finn's thumb brush my hip. "And sex, for that matter. And you know what? Yes. I'm done with fun. You don't get to judge me for that."

I pull away from the table, prepared to leave this place.

Prepared to walk away from the best night I've had in weeks. Months. Maybe years.

Some instinct has me looking back. I glance in

time to see Finn push the entire stack of chips, both the ones we started with and the ones I won, to the dealer. "Keep them," he says.

The dealer's eyes light up. "Sir."

Tears prick my eyes. I feel young and naive, even though I know that's ludicrous. Like I really have been sleeping in a forest for a hundred years. And when awakened by Prince Charming, I discovered that he was a billionaire bachelor named Finn Hughes.

When I climb the stairs, there are more people in which to hide.

I plunge into the crowd, hoping he can't catch me.

Maybe I can call an Uber. My driver would be faster, but I don't want anyone catching wind of this. Not my parents. My mother would be thrilled to know I spent the evening with Finn. It's more my overprotective brothers who'd give me shit.

A man stumbles into my path.

For a moment it seems like an accident. I even reach out, as if to help steady him. He seems drunk. Then he turns his eyes on me, full of interest, and I realize it wasn't an accident. He grabs my wrist and pulls me toward the back wall. I fight him, but not hard enough. I'm still shocked this is happening.

"Come on, darling. I'll pay more than the house, and I'll be done faster, too."

It takes me a long moment to realize he thinks I'm a prostitute. Are there house escorts in addition to the cocktail waitresses?

"Let go of me," I say, yanking, panicking.

Then there's a sharp sound, and I'm free.

The man stumbles away, his back hitting the wall. He holds his arm protectively.

Finn is in front of me. "You made a mistake. Apologize."

"Fuck, I'm sorry. I didn't know she was paid for already."

"Apologize to the lady."

Whatever he sees in Finn's eyes makes him flush. "I'm sorry, ma'am."

After a long, tense moment, Finn nods. Men with bald heads and black suits emerge from the crowd and drag the man out the back door. They must have come when they heard a commotion, but they waited for Finn to decide what to do with the man.

Would they have let Finn hurt him?

That's the power of the Hughes name. I shiver.

Finn is handsome and charming, but it would

be a mistake to underestimate him.

He turns to me as the crowd returns to their games. "Are you okay?"

"Yes," I say, raising my chin so he believes me. The grip on my forearm will probably leave a bruise. But I have long-sleeved clothes to hide it. Having a childhood like mine made me tough enough to withstand some random asshole.

He takes my arm in his, surprisingly gentle. Two fingers brush along the skin that's screaming in pain right now. It was crushed and twisted in that man's fist. "I should find him and kill him for you."

Another shiver runs through me. "Please. I have enough testosterone to deal with between my father and my brothers."

Finn lifts my arm and lowers his head. He places a featherlight kiss on the place where a yellow-blue bruise will be tomorrow. "I'm sorry I didn't get to you sooner."

My throat closes. A violent man couldn't shake me, but kindness can.

So this is what it feels like to be taken care of.

Strange. Scary. Addictive.

"Time to pack up," someone shouts, and then there's melee.

Finn drags me against his body, shielding me

from the crush. The players shove chips into pockets and purses. The dealers slam a lid on the table's banks in what appears to be a practiced move. It's happening so fast I can barely take it in.

"What's happening?" I ask.

The commotion swallows my words, but Finn sees them on my lips. "The cops are coming," he says. "Someone called in a raid. We've got to go."

Chapter Four

Finn

I HALF-CARRY EVA Morelli out the back door.

If she berated me the whole way, I wouldn't blame her. Instead she laughs. It's a wild laugh. A sexy laugh. The kind you make when you're diving off a high cliff.

We're in my car and peeling away from the parking lot as siren lights come into view. Blue and red lights bounce off bricks. They aren't after the patrons. The real goal of these raids is to catch the mysterious Miss M, the woman who owns the underground casino.

It still wouldn't be good to get caught in their net.

Eva Morelli in city lockup? It would be a travesty, but she doesn't look worried. Or pissed that I gave her such a close call. Instead she looks exhilarated.

This.

This is what she'd look like when she's seconds from coming, her cheeks flushed, her eyes sparkling, her hand tight on my arm. I don't know if she even realizes she's still touching me. It's like she's holding on for dear life, and fuck, it feels good.

Then her smile dims. "No one will get hurt, will they?"

Such a caretaker.

If I told her people might get hurt, she'd probably demand I turn the car around.

"Those are some of the wealthiest people in the world. The cops aren't going to risk getting slapped with major lawsuits. They'll be careful if anyone gets caught… which might not even happen. Raids aren't common, but they happen enough that people know the drill."

"Okay." She sits back in the low-slung bucket seat. Her hands go to her cheeks, as if checking that she's still intact. "Okay," she says again.

"Underground gambling. Running from the cops. You're a regular rebel."

She gives a delicate snort. "For two hours, maybe."

"For two hours, so far," I amend. "The night

isn't over yet."

One eyebrow rises. "Haven't you ever heard of quitting while you're ahead?"

"That's not how I play, Eva. I'd rather double down."

That earns me an eye roll. "You're such a smooth talker."

"Do you prefer it rough?" I ask, my tone innocent.

She gives me a glare across the stick shift that I assume is supposed to be intimidating. I just find it sexy. I want her to look at me that way while she rides me. I want her to challenge me to make her come while she tries her best not to.

God, victory will be sweet.

Except I'm not going to make her come.

She's not going to ride me.

Not tonight. And probably not ever if she knows what's good for her. It's just as well that she's not known for one-night stands. That way I won't be tempted.

Right, Hughes. Keep telling yourself that.

Eva Morelli isn't the kind of woman you fuck and walk away from.

She's the kind of woman you keep.

And me? I'm a Hughes. Whether we love them or not, we sure as hell leave them.

One way or the other.

It takes her a couple blocks to realize we're heading north instead of east.

Her gaze goes to me. "Your house?"

Something pangs in my heart. My house. She's not asking if she's going to take a tour of the Hughes estate. She's asking whether I'm going to seduce her.

I don't take women to my home.

The idea of Eva there makes my chest feel tight.

"My yacht."

A smile twitches her lips. "Your yacht."

"Surely you've heard of them. Your family owns several."

"Is this how you impress the ladies?"

"I don't need a large boat to impress the ladies. I already have a very large—"

"Thank you, Mr. Hughes. That will be all."

"I was going to say very large jet skis," I say, all innocence. "Though I do appreciate the way you got all hot schoolteacher on me. All prim and commanding. It will be that much more fun when I finally bend you over the desk."

A gasp. And then a laugh. "You *are* a rascal."

"That might be the right word," I admit. "Even if it is a hundred years old."

"Along with rogue."

"Scoundrel."

"Ne'er do well."

"I do certain things very well, actually."

She gives me a reluctant grin. Then her eyes go wide. "That's yours?"

"I told you it was a yacht."

"That's not a yacht. It's a freaking cruise ship."

She exaggerates. A little bit. It's a custom-built superyacht with two pools, a hot tub, a glass bottom, an IMAX theater, and a crew of twenty. They're not here. The boat is quiet on the water as I hand Eva out of the car.

"Not that one," I tell her, leading her past the craft used for events to the fifty-foot bluewater sailing yacht. It's the one I take when I want a long, peaceful ride through the ocean. It also offers some of the best views of the stars in Bishop's Landing.

I climb aboard and then help her make the hop to the deck.

She wobbles a little in my arms, and my hands immediately go around her waist. I steady her in a split second, but I hold her for several heartbeats after that. Her eyelashes brush her cheeks. Demure? Nervous? Then she glances at me, and I see something else entirely.

A fiery passion that's been banked for years.

Heat rushes through my body in implicit answer.

I force myself to let her go, except for a loose link of our hands. The boat isn't in motion, but it sways gently. I don't want her tumbling overboard. I lead her to the back, where a platform can be used for boarding or sunbathing.

I throw down a couple of outdoor pillows, making us a nest.

Then I pull her down with me.

After an initial stiffness, she relaxes against my side. I'm stretched out flat on the deck, my arm around her. My gaze is on the sky, instead of her, but somehow that makes this moment feel more intimate. I run playful fingertips down her arm, teasing out more goosebumps.

"Beautiful," she says, looking at the stars.

When you lie down like this, you feel insignificant. That's what I like about it. Like I'm a speck of cosmic dust. Like the fate of my entire family, as well as several thousand other families, doesn't rest on my shoulders.

I look down at Eva's face in profile—her strong brow, her faintly upturned nose, her full lips. Her black silky hair tickles my nose.

"Beautiful," I murmur in agreement.

Her dark gaze meets mine. "Thank you for tonight."

"For almost getting you arrested?"

"For taking pity on me. I know that's why you did it."

I don't pretend not to understand. "Alex fucking Langley."

She makes a face. "I mean, he's nice. But going to my mom instead of me, the whole arranged-match thing...I hate it. I'm sure you must get that, too."

"Something like that."

There's a ticking clock where I'm concerned.

Get married while you still can, my mother implies with every society chick she introduces me to. I've already told her I'm not getting married.

And I'm sure as hell not having children. Not ever.

I wouldn't do that to them.

"At least he's honest about what he wants. In a way that's better than someone asking me out and charming me as if they want...you know. A real relationship."

"What's wrong with being charming?"

"I don't like charming men," she says, earnest.

It makes me grin. "Everyone likes charming

men."

"I want a real relationship with you," I say, my voice low in the style of a confession.

Her eyes are as luminous as the night sky. "Do you?"

The words are hard to get out. "I can't have it."

Because of my family's secrets.

I don't get that with anyone. Especially not a woman like her.

Hurt ricochets through her eyes. She gives a short nod that doesn't quite hide the pain.

I've never been tempted to tell anyone before, but part of me wants to do that now. *It's not you, it's me. It's not you, it's my family. It's not you, it's a modern-day curse.*

"Do you know any of them?" she says, gesturing upward. "The stars?"

"A sailor has to know. That bright spot right there? That isn't a star. That's Jupiter."

She squints.

"And to the right… there's the Lion. And the one right above it, that's Denebola. It's bigger and brighter than the sun. And it's the tail star in Leo. Like your brother."

"Like my brother," she repeats, her words slow and thoughtful. "He's going to have so many questions when my mom tells everyone that I left the gala with you."

"Tell him to mind his own business."

She laughs a little. "No one tells Leo Morelli what to do."

Everyone knows the Morelli brothers are overprotective bastards. Which makes their sisters off-limits unless you're willing to run the gauntlet. I wouldn't let that stop me. I have my own reasons for keeping this casual. "Besides, Sarah Morelli isn't going to tell anyone about one little joyride."

"Oh, she's already told everyone at the gala. I'm sure."

I wince, acknowledging she's probably right. Which means my mother will hear about it. She's no fan of the Morellis, but she's desperate enough to want me married and producing offspring that she'd probably accept it.

"I'll set her straight," Eva says, as if offering reassurance.

As if I'm so intent on bachelorhood that I'd be offended at a rumor. "You know my theory on this. Double down. Convince her we flew to Vegas and eloped."

"Don't," she says, laughing. "She'll start naming our children."

The idea of children makes my smile fade. "Does it matter?"

Eva looks uncertain. "What?"

"What she thinks? Does it matter? Let her believe what she wants."

"Finn."

"I mean it." I lift up on an elbow, resting her head on my forearm. We aren't touching anywhere beneath the belt, but it's still a sexual position. This is how I'd look down at her if I was thrusting inside her, making her moan. I'd lean down and nip her sensitive throat. I'd make her gasp and beg and—No, I won't do any of that. "We can pretend."

"*What?*"

"Let her think we're dating. If she thinks you're already seeing someone, she won't push you to marry Alex fucking Langley. Or anyone else. At least for a while."

"She wouldn't keep it a secret. She'd tell absolutely everyone. Everyone in Bishop's Landing, everyone in New York, maybe everyone in the world."

"So let her. We would know what the truth is."

"But it's not real."

"Who cares what people think? It will get her

off your back."

She looks back at the stars. Her profile makes her look regal. Like a queen. "And it would get your parents off your back, too, right? It would work both ways."

"Right," I say, though I don't care as much what my mother says.

Nothing, absolutely no amount of coaxing or browbeating, would ever convince me to marry. It's not just a personal preference. It's a question of ethics. I'd never saddle a woman with someone like me.

Then she turns to look at me. Her expression steals my breath away. She's stunning. She's always looked this way, hasn't she? At balls and galas. At charity dinners. She's always been an untouchable goddess, only I get to touch her right now.

For as long as we're fake dating, I'll get to keep touching her.

"Okay," she says, her tone resolute.

"Okay?"

"I'll pretend to date you."

"Thank God," I say, and then I can't help it. I kiss her. It starts off as a brush of lips. It turns into more. I nibble her full lips, and she opens them on a gasp. A question and answer. A seeking and a solace. She smells so good. I want to inhale her again and again, until my lungs are full, until she pervades every part of my being.

I want to take the kiss deeper. To explore her fully.

Instead I force myself to pull back. "To seal the agreement," I manage in a hoarse voice.

Her lids are still heavy, her dark eyes hazy with pleasure. After a long moment they clear. She searches my expression for something. I don't know what she finds, but it makes her nod.

Then she pulls me down for another kiss. Her lips are soft and welcoming. They promise comfort at the end of a hard day. They feel like poetry written on concrete, incongruous beauty in a harsh, barren landscape. She's the one who takes the kiss deeper. Her tongue darts out, curious. A little playful. And I reward her with a gentle, explicit suck. *This is what I want to do to your clit,* I say with touch instead of words. *You taste so fucking good.*

I'm struck with the thought that I might not be able to stop.

That I might be out here on the deck of my boat for the rest of eternity, kissing Eva Morelli. Even when the sun rises, even when it sets again, even when fall comes, even when the boat sails away for some vacation or other, I might still be here kissing her.

Everyone else can handle their own shit.

It's an absurd notion. I have too much to do. I have responsibilities. My family depends on me. The company depends on me. The secrets definitely depend on me.

And if I waited here long enough, if I kissed her for long enough, she would know.

That is the problem with forever.

I already know how it ends.

Chapter Five

Eva

SOMEONE'S KNOCKING ON the door.

That's the only thought that enters my deep sleep. I pull a pillow over my head, wanting to prolong the dream. To remain in the place where Finn Hughes kissed me and kissed me until I was nothing but an exposed nerve of need.

Knock. Knock. Knock.

The doorman would only let up someone in my family.

And if they're showing up at—I squint at the alarm clock—six in the morning, that means they need help. That thought propels me into action. I throw on a silk robe over my nightgown and pad to the door.

My eyesight is still a little fuzzy, but I recognize my sister through the peephole.

I open the door. "What's wrong?"

My youngest sister looks pale and worried. "*Eva.*"

She throws herself at me, and I catch her in my arms. I haven't held her like this since she was a child, and I was comforting her after a nightmare. "Lizzy. What on earth?"

She pulls away and seems to notice my state of undress. "Did I wake you up? Oh my God. I did. I'll go. I can come back later."

"Don't even think about it." I guide her to the settee. My loft is a little eclectic, something that drives my mother insane. There are jewel tones and interesting textures. The occasional stamp of whimsy. All of it seems superfluous now. I sit down beside her and hold her hands. "Now tell me what's going on."

She looks absolutely stricken. "Don't freak out."

Of course my immediate reaction is to freak out. Internally. But I have a lot of practice with a poker face. Not the kind you use in an underground casino. The kind you use when your family is coming apart at the seams and you're the only one who can hold them together.

"Whatever it is, we'll figure it out. Okay? I promise."

"I think I might be pregnant."

The words come out garbled. *IthinkImightbepregnant.*

They take a moment to fully understand. I can feel the blood drain from my face, but I maintain my poise.

"Have you taken a test?" I manage to ask.

"No, but I'm late. My period, I mean. It usually shows up like clockwork, but it's been six days, and there's been no sign of it. I don't know what to do."

Six days late. Not a good sign for someone who's regular. Not proof of anything, either. It might be a false alarm. "I'm glad you came to me. We'll take a test, and then we'll know for sure."

"But what if…"

"We'll figure it out," I remind her. "I promise."

A discordant cheerful ring comes from my bedroom. My phone.

This is more important than any phone call except… what if someone else in my family needs me? It's still early to be calling about nothing.

"Stay here," I say, squeezing Lizzy's hand. "I'll be right back, and then we'll do this together."

I dash into my bedroom, already thinking about where I can find a pregnancy test. There are none in my loft, that's for sure. Maybe I can call down to the concierge. It's a full-service condo, so they'll bring me groceries or lattes.

Or pregnancy tests, most likely.

I dig through the clutch I used last night. My hand lands on something foreign. I pull out a handful of heavy, round poker chips. They must have fallen inside during play. Or maybe Finn slipped them inside. It brings the night before into crystal-clear focus.

Not a dream, then.

Am I really fake dating Finn Hughes?

I dig through the chips until I find it: the quarter he gave me. *If you have a good time tonight, then I win. But if you, in your honest assessment, don't have a good time, you win.*

Now I owe him twenty-five cents.

My mom's frozen smiling face appears on my phone.

"Hey."

"I can't believe you didn't text me, at least. How did it go?"

"How did what go?" I peek back into the living room. Lizzy twists her hands together. I wish I could offer her more reassurance, but fuck. *Fuck.* If she's pregnant, this is going to be a shitshow. My parents will lose their Catholic minds. My brothers will probably start a war with whoever the father is. This is about to be a circus.

"Your *plans*," my mother says, impatient. "Your plans with Finn Hughes. I can't imagine why you didn't tell me about them. And why you made him search the mansion for you."

He wasn't really searching for me.

The words are on the tip of my tongue.

He only took pity on me because you wanted me to marry Alex Langley.

I could explain to Finn that our little game of pretend was a bad idea, after all.

And then I'd have no excuse to see him again.

No excuse to kiss him again.

"It was a fun date," I say, my heart pounding.

"A date?" My mother sounds like she's about to blast into orbit. "I wasn't sure. The way he looked at you… but of course he did. You're beautiful. Accomplished. And way too good for Alex Langley. A Hughes, Eva. That's wonderful."

"We're just seeing each other," I add hastily. "It probably won't turn into anything."

"If you play your cards right, it can turn into everything."

I glance down at the quarter in my hand. "I'm serious. We're together, but in a very shallow, non-commitment, Tinder-hookup kind of way."

She ignores this, of course. "You only have to keep him enthralled through the courtship. Compliment him. Please him. Make him feel like a big, strong man."

"Gross, Mom."

"At least until you get a ring on your finger."

"I can't imagine why I've resisted marriage so far."

"You have to bring him to dinner."

"Maybe. Mom, I have to go. There's a… thing I have to do." Starting with finding a pregnancy test for my baby sister. And ending with making sure Finn is still in agreement about the fake dating. Last night still seems like a faraway fever dream.

I force my way off the phone and call down to concierge.

A few tense minutes later there's a knock at the door. Goddard is the oldest concierge. He gives me a kind look and an unmarked paper bag. "Thank you," I say, handing over a tip.

"Any time, Ms. Morelli."

As soon as the door is closed, Lizzy traps herself inside the bathroom with the box.

Five minutes pass. "Liz?"

Her shout comes through the door. "It says I have to wait!"

Another ten minutes pass. "Lizzy?"

"Not yet!"

"Lisbetta Anne-Marie Morelli, open this door."

Her voice is muffled this time. And thick with misery. "It's unlocked."

I open the door to find her sitting on the floor, her back to the wall, her head in her hands. "I can't look at it. I'm going to throw up."

I pick up the little test, not caring that my sister peed on it a few minutes ago. There's only one line. My heart thuds. I read the instructions—once, twice, three times. Just to be sure.

There would be two lines if she were pregnant.

No lines if the test were broken.

One line means she's definitely not pregnant. *Oh, thank God.* That's what I want to say out loud. Instead I force myself to say a calm, casual, nonjudgmental, "Negative."

"Are you sure?" Then my sister jumps up. She does the same thing I did, reading the little instruction packet to be sure. "Oh my God. It's negative. Oh my *God.*"

Then she bursts into tears.

I guide her back to the settee, where I comfort her until her heart-wrenching sobs turn into little whimpers. Then I guide her gently into my guest bedroom, where I tuck her in a ridiculous amount of blankets. I turn on the sound machine and set the fan to high. I make sure the drapes are closed tight so that no morning light can seep in. Then I look down at her. She's already sleeping. There are faint shadows under her eyes. How much sleep has she lost worrying about this? I lean down to give her forehead a kiss. I know she's technically an adult now, but I can't help treating her like the precocious little girl from years ago.

Part of me wants to wake her up and demand to know who had sex with her.

The more sane part of me knows that she already has four overprotective brothers. She doesn't also need an overprotective sister. There's a reason she came to me. Because she knew that somehow I would keep a cool head.

I return to the living room and stand there for probably far too long.

It's been a strange twelve hours.

Another knock at the door. "You've got to be kidding me," I mutter.

It's my brother Leo, the one closest to me in age, standing in the hallway with a curious expression on his face. With black hair and dark eyes, he's a quintessential Morelli. All of us got that from our father. My mother's red hair and green eyes stand out whenever she's in a family photo. Though I can see the shape of her eyes in my brother.

He's dressed for the office. "Hey."

I lead him into the kitchen and start coffee. That's for him. I prefer my caffeine in the form of Diet Coke. He goes to my fridge and pulls out a can, which he hands to me the moment I turn away from the coffee.

"Don't make too much noise. Lizzy's here."

He glances toward the bedroom. "What's wrong?"

"Nothing," I say, because he doesn't need to know about the pregnancy scare. It's true that we share pretty much everything. We also came together to protect the other siblings from our dad's drunken rages. If Lizzy were actually pregnant, this would turn into a strategy session. But since it was negative, he doesn't need to know.

The heart palpitations alone cannot be safe.

He looks skeptical. "She slept over?"

"If you must know, she was worried about starting college. She came over and had a little emotional breakdown, and I put her to bed."

"Damn it. Does she need a tutor? A pep talk?

Does she need—"

"All she needs is a good day's sleep. Shouldn't you be at work right now?" Or at home. Ever since his marriage he's been pretty much glued to his wife, Haley's, side. Finding out she's pregnant only made him ten times more clingy. I don't know how she deals with him.

"I'll be at work soon enough. And I need you to come to the office this week. I have papers that need your signature."

I crack open the Diet Coke. It's cold, bubbly, and most importantly, reliable. "You know, you should give Haley my seat on the advisory board. She's your wife."

"I want *you* on the advisory board. That's why you're on it."

"But Haley—"

"Haley wants to write stories. She has no interest in my business."

"Who said I had any interest in it?"

"Please. You love giving endowments to God knows who."

"You would know who if you bothered to read my quarterly reports."

"I do read them, sister mine. Which is how I know you can read a balance sheet and manage a high-stakes project better than anyone on my payroll."

This is an old argument. I've done work for Leo, before the foundation was up and running. And I was fine with inheriting Leo's business when he wasn't married. It's more than inheritance. I would be the acting CEO. It would have been an extension of my work for the family. But now that he's married, he has his own beautiful family. His own heirs. "How's Haley? I haven't texted her in a few days."

"Tired." For a split second, worry crosses his face. Then it's gone, as if he slipped it into his pocket like a wallet. Out of sight. "Uncomfortable. And she still has two months to go."

"You never got back to me about the menu."

"That's because her taste changes every single day. Yesterday she wanted peaches. Only peaches. God forgive the chef who tried to give her a peach and blueberry cobbler. You would have thought blueberries were poison."

"Then it's all the more important that I have a list of what she likes to eat."

"Then I get a text on the way here." He pulls out his phone, because my brother isn't above a little theater. He reads off the screen. "*What's that thing with the melty cheese?* This was before seven a.m. So I ask if she means fondue, which I thought was a reasonable guess."

I nod, unable to hold back my smile. "Of course it was."

"No, she says. The one with the melted cheese on top. So I tell her Croque Monsieur. Rarebit. French onion soup. I must have named fifty things with melted cheese on top."

"Was it nachos?"

"How the hell did you figure it out?"

"Sympathy hormones," I say with a light laugh. "I'm just thinking about what I'd want if I were super pregnant. And I can probably serve nachos at the baby shower."

"Don't bother. I had the executive chef of Merida make her something for lunch."

"The man has Michelin stars, Leo."

"And he was happy to make a pregnant woman something she craved. He was especially happy when he saw the generous investment I made in his restaurant."

My brother's love for his wife is over the top, which is beautiful to watch. Terrifying to experience. Risky. Dangerous, when you're a teenage girl caught in a game with a much older man. I shake away my past. "You're taking good care of her."

He looks pensive. "I hope so."

"She's lucky to have you."

He gives me a pointed look. "I heard you went out with Finn Hughes last night."

"Mom exaggerates. You know that."

"I didn't hear it from Mom. I heard it from a friend. Someone who was in an underground casino, who thought he saw my sister. No, I told him. My sister would never go to an illegal club that got raided by the police."

My cheeks heat. "Don't freak out," I say, echoing Lizzy's words.

He gives me a dire expression. "Eva."

"Finn and I hung out. It was no big deal. Really."

"He's a player."

"You think I don't know that? He's a good time. I'm not expecting anything different. But you should know something. We might be…pretend dating."

A slow blink. "Come again?"

"We might be *pretending* that we're *dating*."

"I might be having a stroke. Are you dating Finn Hughes or not?"

I roll my eyes. "It's a fake thing, just to get Mom off my back about Alex Langley."

"What about Langley?"

"She tried to set me up with him. Apparently

he's done mourning his late wife and ready to find a new baby-making machine. And like she said, I'm not getting any younger."

His expression turns dark. "I'll talk to her."

"No, don't. I can handle her. And this whole Finn thing should get her off my back for a while anyway. I'll let her dream about wedding colors for a while before we break up."

"Daphne's wedding colors aren't enough?"

"Nothing's enough for Mom."

"Christ."

"It's not a big deal."

"Are you okay, Eva? Seriously?"

I swallow around the knot in my throat. Leo knows what I was like at my lowest. He knows about the heartbreak. About the way it swallowed me whole. I lived in a state of waking slumber for a long time after that.

You could say that I was still in it when I was at the gala last night.

And I was woken with a kiss.

Chapter Six

Finn

Escape sounds like Eva Morelli laughing with joy when she gets a full house.

Reality sounds like dishes clanging in the kitchen and indistinct yelling.

I drop my coat and my briefcase right there in the foyer and stride toward the sounds.

My father stands in the middle of a disaster, arguing with a nurse about what he'll eat. The nurse deals with him patiently and faintly pleading. This must have been going on for a while. A questionable splat of red on the wall is probably the remains of spaghetti sauce.

An onion is half chopped on the butcher block counter. A puddle of butter lounges in an empty skillet. Eggs roll, still complete in their shells, on the floor. Somehow they didn't crack when they fell. A minor miracle.

My father loved to cook. I suppose that shouldn't be in the past tense. He still loves to cook. And I would be happy to let him, if he could be trusted with knives and hot metal.

"Dad," I say, coming to hold his shoulders. "What's wrong?"

"She keeps giving me dinner. It's breakfast time. I tried to tell her."

We don't argue with him about the time. It won't convince him, and there's no point. If he doesn't want spaghetti, he doesn't have to eat it. "What would you like to eat?"

"An omelet. I can make it. I can make it myself." He tries to pull away, toward the half-chopped onion. "You have to tell that woman I can make an omelet, for God's sake."

Jennifer Brown has been one of his nurses for years. He can't remember her name. Someday he won't remember my name, either. She turns her back, wiping a perfectly clean counter from far away. She's giving us privacy, but she's also staying nearby in case I need help. For the most part I deal with my father when I'm home. Occasionally, if he fights long and hard, I have to stop him. It's for his own safety.

"I can make you an omelet," I say, my tone

gentle.

We learned early about sundowning. It's when an older person gets confused and argumentative at night. "You're a good boy, but you could burn toast."

My laugh is soft and soundless. It's true that I'm not much of a cook. I've picked up a few basic skills in the years since I've been a boy, though. "Then Jennifer can make you an omelet. She does it the way you like, nice and fluffy."

He gives her a suspicious look. "Why is she here? Where's Geneva?"

A knot forms in my throat. He asks after her every day. There's no good answer, but I've tried them all. "She's out right now. A gala. Would you like Jennifer to make you an omelet? I see onions there. What else? Cheddar cheese? Spinach?"

"I can make it," he insists.

"Dad."

"Why doesn't anyone trust me? I'm the master of my own home, aren't I? I'm a grown man, aren't I? How dare you tell me what to do. I ought to ground you for the week. If I were your father I'd turn you around and whip your bottom bloody."

"Dad, stop."

"Stop telling me what to do!"

He yanks away with sudden force, and I let him go. It's always a struggle, how hard to hold him. It's cruel to treat him as a prisoner, but it's negligent to let him hurt himself.

The area between those is a large expanse of gray.

It seems to take him by surprise, the fact that he's midflight.

He stumbles back. *Crack.* An egg turns to mush beneath his bare foot.

He looks down, confused. "Why are there eggs on the floor?"

Jennifer sweeps back in. My father allows her to guide him to the chair. She fusses over him, and he turns passive as she cleans the egg off his foot.

I grab a box of mix from the pantry. "Pancakes."

My father blinks. "Pancakes?"

"I can make pancakes, at the very least. They won't be too burned."

"Geneva likes them that way."

My mother does prefer pancakes well done. At least, she did before she stopped eating carbs. She loved when the butter turned crisp at the edges. Dad used to give her a hard time about it, but of course he'd cook them the way she liked.

He'd tease her about it, back when there was still laughter in this house.

The mix is the easy kind. I only need to add water. When the pan is hot, I pour the lumpy batter in the center and wait for little bubbles to rise to the top.

"What do you want to drink?" Jennifer asks.

There's no frustration in her voice. She's a wonderful caregiver. Skilled. Patient. And most important for this position, discreet. I don't feel guilty because she's paid a lot of money to do it. That, along with my recommendation, allowed her to purchase one of the smaller homes on the west end of Bishop's Landing. Her salary put her two sons through Harvard.

Not bad for a single mom who went to night school to become a nurse.

"Orange juice?" she suggests. "Or how about a glass of milk?" We're both going along with the morning routine, because it's easier than arguing. There's only one tough thing about mornings—

"I want coffee."

"Mr. Hughes," she says, soothing.

"No, make it a flat white. I need a pick-me-up to face the day."

Even if it were morning, we wouldn't give him coffee. And definitely not espresso. Caffeine makes him more querulous. We don't even keep a Keurig in the house. If I want to drink coffee, I do it at the office so he doesn't see.

I slide a plate with two pancakes toward him. "Extra syrup. The way you like it."

He frowns down at the plate. Then he looks outside, where it's shadowed. Like the dawn, I suppose, but there's a heavier quality to it that speaks of evening in summer.

"What time is it, Phineas?" he demands, his eyes huge, sorrowful.

"It's morning, Dad," I say, handing him the syrup pitcher. It's an antique piece from the eighteen hundreds, ceramic with a profusion of red and orange flowers hand-painted across. We once had a set of two. A memory comes to me—Dad throwing the other one. A crash of white ceramic and bold paint against the wall, right where the spaghetti Jennifer cooked remains.

"What do you have planned today?" I ask.

"A lot of meetings." He sighs. "I swear some days are all meetings, and no work."

He starts listing names, but they're not anyone who works at the family company now. They're not his business partners from the present. They're all old business partners from twenty years ago, when he was a young man, just starting out. His first business partners.

Some of them are friends he has at the golf club.

"That sounds good, Dad. Real good."

"I might sign a deal. Now that's a good meeting, when you sign a deal. Ink on paper. Makes the world go round, son."

This is the game that I play with my father. It's the act we repeat over and over again. He tells me about a fictional life, and I pretend it's real. One of his doctors told me to do that early on. I was trying to tell my dad the facts. Trying to make him understand.

The doctor took me aside and said, "Don't. It's stressful for you, and it's stressful for him. Whatever he says, agree with it."

I had been upset. "So I should pretend?"

"It's not really pretending, because it's real for him," she said.

"Where are the properties?" I ask him now.

He proceeds to tell me about a new development near the Palisades, a small collection of private homes. "Not as lucrative as condos, of course. But they'll keep the view clean."

Dad cares about things like clean views. And clean air. It's a form of noblesse oblige for him. Despite his rigorous work schedule and his social commitments, every few weekends we'd go down to Bear Mountain. We'd take a dusty Range Rover and fishing poles as props. *These people depend on you,* he'd say, gesturing to the families packed in the public parks. *Even more than the politicians they vote for. It's not only our employees who rely on Hughes Industries. The entire economy depends on what we do.*

Then we'd return home to the billion-dollar Hughes estate.

"I have to check on a few things," I tell him. "Will you be all right?"

"Of course." He waves me off. "Go finish your homework."

I was only eight years old when we'd have those talks, but he had to start early. Because that's what the disease does. Even then it was eating away at his brain.

By the time I was sixteen I was running Hughes Industries.

I manage the empire my father's father passed down to him.

And I do it well.

It's not pride that makes me say that. There's proof. There are profits and expanding companies. Mergers. Celebrations. Retirement parties in the conference room. It doesn't really matter if I would have wanted something different. I've been groomed for this role since I was in preschool. Even then, my father knew what his fate would be.

He knew that he'd forget everything.

His knowledge of business. The company of friends. His wife. All of them, gone by the time he was thirty. Oh, he's still the CEO publicly. He just works from home. I'm the one who goes into the office. I have access to both of our email addresses. I can forge his signature as well as mine. I bring him into the office every six months to shake hands and wave, as proof of life.

That same fate awaits me. Early onset dementia has run in the family for generations. Awareness of my downfall is never far from my mind.

Of course, I wasn't only taught to run the business.

I was taught that I needed to marry and produce an heir. Someone who I could train from their toddler years to take over the Hughes empire. Our entire extended family depends on it. Tens of thousands of employees depend on it. The economy depends on it.

Except I refuse.

I'm not going to saddle any woman with my

ticking time bomb of a brain. I'm not going to bring another soul into this world with disease embedded in their body. It ends with me. No, I'll raise my brother. That's the only legacy I'll leave behind. The family, the employees, the economy—they'll have to fend for themselves.

I'm not going to force someone else to maintain the charade that is my life.

It's all fake, which is perfect for me.

I have a hundred things to do for Hughes Industries tonight before I go to bed. Another hundred things to do starting tomorrow at 5 am. But all I can think about is Eva Morelli.

She is beautiful with those sad eyes and tragic secrets.

I don't like charming men.

What is she hiding? I have no right to ask, not with my own secrets.

It doesn't take me long to find her email address. It was already in my inbox, tacked on to a group message from last year to the donors of a Bishop's Landing fundraiser. Someone forgot to put them in BCC.

Eva,

You. Me. Dinner tomorrow night at 8 o'clock.

—Finn

I'm already knee deep in a balance sheet when I get a ding on my phone.

Finn,

I wasn't sure you were serious about fake dating.

—Eva

I answer.

Eva,

The first rule of fake dating is you don't put it in writing.

Also: dead serious.

—Finn

P.S. Tell your mother.

CHAPTER SEVEN

Eva

TECHNICALLY SPEAKING, I have a job.

I'm the Director of the Morelli Fund, an organization dedicated to helping families. You wouldn't think it was a full-time job to give away millions of dollars every year, but it is. In the wrong hands that money would be wasted, or worse, embezzled. Finding organizations with both the integrity and the framework in place to make use of the money takes time.

And despite taking care of my parents and my siblings, despite the galas and the dinner parties and the brunches, despite the merciless whir of my life, I have time.

Finn said he knows what I'm worth. It's not a small number. Most of the money comes from my parents in a trust that pays out annually.

More money than I could ever spend.

Then there's the property. Leo gave me a deed for my nineteenth birthday. It was a rundown duplex, but the start of an empire. He wanted to build it himself, not relying on family money. He gives me property every year.

For my thirty-third birthday he gifted me a cottage in Vail.

The word *cottage* is a joke. It has an infinity pool and stunning panoramic views. Nestled on top of its own little mountain, it's worth a cool four million dollars.

I could sell some of the properties, of course. But I don't. They have sentimental value. Some, like the condo in Reykjavík and the villa on the Amalfi coast, I rent out using a management service. Others, like the cottage, I keep for personal use.

But my loft in New York City came from a different place.

I inherited it when I was nine years old.

My great-aunt was what they called an Original. She was vivacious and unpredictable. I admired her from the time I was born. In a family that valued appearances and morality, she was a breath of fresh air. I would run through her penthouse in Tribeca whenever we visited. Mom would admonish me to be careful. "Don't break the art," she said, giving a sideways glance to a white ceramic statue of nymphs cavorting through reeds. It took pride of place beneath a chandelier made of origami cranes. Priceless oriental art nestled among handmade and thrift shop finds. Nothing was labeled. Much of it was strange. And everything was interesting.

When she passed away of cancer, I was heartbroken.

Her loft became my haven.

I maintain my old bedroom in my parents' house. There's even a designated suite for me in Leo's mansion, but this has been my true home since I was a child. It's where I spend most of my time, even where I do most of my work. The fund has official space within Morelli Holdings, but it's easier and less intimidating for people to meet with me at home.

Today that includes a pitch from a charity that helps LGBTQ+ youth who are in crisis. Of course the cause is worthy. That's how they got an appointment with me. My job is to make sure they have the structures in place to provide care. They've come with a PowerPoint and a glossy printed plan for how they can spend five million dollars in the next three years.

I narrow my eyes at the final estimates. "What about infrastructure costs?"

The director of the charity frowns down at her chart. "I'm sure that's covered in the startup analysis. Or maybe somewhere else."

"I want to see confirmation of that. And a breakdown of that section."

"Of course, Ms. Morelli. Thank you so much for the opportunity. We're so grateful for the chance to speak with you. We hope you'll consider us."

I stand and shake hands with her before escorting her out.

My phone rings. Half my mind is still on the pitch I just saw. It's a great cause, but I saw the panic in the director's eyes. They may not have included infrastructure. Which might make the entire budget unworkable. Not to mention, it illustrates that they aren't ready for a donation of that size. Times like this break my heart, but we won't turn them down entirely. Instead I'll arrange a smaller donation, something manageable for them.

Which also means we'll be able to help more charities.

I don't give a fuck if Morelli Holdings only donates so that they'll get a tax write-off. We do real good in the world at the fund.

My mind is still on the projections when my phone rings. "Hello?"

"Ms. Morelli," comes a smooth voice over the phone.

I feel my cheeks grow warm. "Mr. Hughes."

"It occurred to me this morning that we had skipped a few steps. An underground casino is all well and good, but what happened to taking a woman out to dinner?"

"Is that an invitation?"

A low laugh answers me. "Is that a yes?"

It's been a long time since I've flirted like this. And the last time was so furtive, tinged with guilt and shame and eventually heartache, that it bore little resemblance to this.

"I thought you might be tired of me," I say lightly.

"Never. And besides, if we're going to pull off this fake relationship, we need to be believable. We can cover the basics tonight, like that movie *Green Card*."

"My favorite color is a deep, emerald green."

"I sleep on the left side of the bed."

"There's an old scar on my left knee from when I fell out of a tree. My father grounded Leo for a month for making that rope ladder."

"The only food I'm allergic to is chamomile, something I found out during an unfortunate visit to a Michelin-starred restaurant who made chamomile panna cotta."

My heart feels full with the momentum of the moment. "So would the date be a pretend date or a real date?"

"A pretend date," he answers promptly, which makes my stomach sink, even though I should know better. "But it has to appear like a real date."

That's how I find myself agonizing over my dress the next evening.

It shouldn't matter, but it does. He's twenty-nine years old. I'm already older than him. I don't want to dress like someone his mother would be friends with. I shove aside a conservative Dior dress that would look at home at any charity board meeting. Then again, I don't want to appear like I'm trying too hard to appear young. I push past a skintight black dress.

This isn't even a real date.

Ridiculous, Morelli. Get a grip.

This isn't a real date, so I don't have to worry about impressing anyone. That's the magic of a fake relationship. There's no sex, no expectations. No tender kisses beneath the stars, most likely.

That makes me sad. Maybe I don't have to choose between them. Maybe, if Finn is amenable, we could kiss again during this fake relationship.

I flip across to one dress and the next. Nothing works.

Nothing, nothing, nothing.

The doorbell rings. I go and open it and find my sister, Sophia, waiting outside, her arms stuffed with fabric. "Don't despair, sweet sister. I'm here to save you."

"Who even told you?"

"Mom's telling the whole city, naturally."

Part of me wants to tell her the truth. *This isn't a real date. It's pretend.* Then again, the more people who know about it, the more risk there is of discovery. And Sophia isn't precisely known for discretion.

Another part of me wants to know what it would be like to have a real date. Even if it's only pretend, it will have to look real. Maybe it will even feel real.

"My closet looks like a bomb went off."

She pushes sunglasses up on top of her head. "Let's get to work."

I step back. "Thank you for saving me."

"Nooo problem," she says in a singsong voice. Sophia loves fashion. She knows all the designers in New York City and some in Paris. Which means she also has access to their samples, if she asks nicely.

One after another, she arranges the dresses on the bed. "Try this one first."

I go with it into the bathroom and come out a moment later, my face scarlet. "This is way too short."

"Turn around," she says. I do, but I can practically feel it rolling up my ass.

"I can't wear this."

"You look great in it," she says. "But if you think it's too short, try this one."

We go through two more before I find it. The gold wrap dress that accentuates my curves rather than hiding them. I stand in front of the mirror, turning this way and that.

"A power dress," Sophia says with satisfaction.

"Yes," I say, looking at how lush my ass looks right now. "It is a power dress."

She claps her hands. "He's going to freaking die when he sees you."

I give her an impulsive hug. "Thank you for this, sister mine. Seriously."

"Hey. Of course. You do enough for me. For all of us. And it's a rare day when you actually need or want my help. I was happy to do it."

A rare day when you actually need or want my help. I hadn't realized that I'd been so resistant to help. Maybe I do need to get better about accepting support instead of always giving it.

Well, let's not go that far.

But the dress is beautiful.

The doorbell rings, and Sophia goes to answer it.

She comes back with Mama.

The scent of Chanel N°5 hits me before she does. Then I'm wrapped in silk-covered arms, with air kisses on either side of my cheeks. "I had to see you."

"It's not prom."

"It's not every day one of your daughters goes on a date with a Hughes."

Fake date, I hear in my head. It's only a fake date. There's no reason for me to feel so out of my depth with it. It is fake. It just has to look real. We'll go to a real restaurant and eat real food. We might have a real kiss at the end of this night.

"Let me look at you," she says, standing back. "Sophia dressed you? You have an eye, darling. She looks ravishing. I wouldn't have picked it off a rack, but look at her. She's stunning. He won't know what to think."

I've never heard so many kind words from my

mother, one after the other. Oh, she loves her children in her own distracted way. But a loveless marriage and a grueling social status have always taken precedence in her life.

"Thanks, Mom."

I feel almost embarrassed at how much I like myself in this dress.

"There's one more thing," Sophia says.

One more thing turns out to be a bloodred lipstick. She wipes off what I had before and replaces it with a bold, sensual color. It makes me look worldly and brave.

"Are you sure about this?" I ask, even though I can't change it. I can't even look away. That's how impressive the woman standing in front of the mirror looks. It's only a pretend situation, like the date itself, but in this moment it doesn't matter.

When we come out of the bathroom, my mother claps. "Perfect. Now, Eva. You and I have never talked about this before, but if he asks to come for coffee after the date—"

"Mom."

"Are you going to tell her about the birds and the bees?" Sophia asks, looking delighted.

"She has to know," my mother says.

"I'm thirty-three years old."

"There's no need to be embarrassed," she says, her tone soothing. "You've never been interested in boys. In fact, your father wondered if perhaps you were interested in women."

Pain forces my eyes closed. If only they knew that I lost my virginity when I was nineteen. I gave more than my innocence to that man. "I've had sex before."

"Oh." My mother blinks.

"Please don't look so shocked."

"This is fascinating," Sophia says, eyes bright with humor.

"I don't understand why you aren't having this conversation with her," I say, pointing at a sister who's having way too much fun with this.

"Everyone knows Sophia's had sex." My mother.

"Does the scarlet letter on my clothes give it away?" Sophia asks.

I hold up my hands before my family drives me insane. "Listen, I *have* had sex. Which is great, but more importantly, I will *not* be having sex with Finn Hughes. And more important than that, if I was going to have sex, I wouldn't talk to you about it."

"Men like lingerie," my mother says, not even remotely deterred.

"I really don't want to hear this."

"You can't wear it at the restaurant, obviously. But when you bring him back up here, you can say you're going to slip into something more comfortable."

"This sounds like porn," I say.

"Bad porn," Sophia says, wincing.

As if to punctuate that proclamation, the doorbell rings.

Finn looks incredible in his suit. He greets me warmly before turning to my family. "Mrs. Morelli. Sophia. I didn't know you would be here."

"We just dropped by to see our lovely Eva," she says, as if it's random happenstance. "And she told us she had plans with you. Again."

"I do seem to be monopolizing her company. But what good company it is." He grins at me, as if he knows that my sister came here to dress me. And that my mother came here to talk about the birds and the bees. And that, somehow, it's all a joke that we're in on together.

He has that effect.

It's not embarrassing, in this moment. It's effervescent. Like life is a fizzy drink.

"We're going to the new Italian restaurant on the Upper East Side." He gives her a lopsided smile. "Don't worry. I'll have her home by curfew."

"Don't worry about that." Somehow the cheeks of this fifty-something-year-old woman turn red. As if she's remembering our conversation about porn. "I'm sure whatever time you two kids get to bed will be fine."

The word *bed* hangs in the air between us.

Sophia's eyes twinkle with barely suppressed glee.

We go outside to where Finn's car is waiting. He hands me into a Lamborghini. I admire the twinkle of the gold fabric in the moonlight. He returns to his seat and glides onto the road.

"How many cars do you have?" I ask.

"A few."

"One for every day of the month?"

"Not quite that many. Although if I count the cars at other properties…"

That makes me laugh. "So you like cars."

"I like speed," he says. "Cars. And horses."

"Thoroughbreds. I remember."

"Well, did we pull it off? Did your family believe it?"

"Oh, they believed it. They believed it a little too well. If you're not careful, my mother is going to find a way to trap you in a real relationship."

"A shotgun wedding?"

"You'd have to get me pregnant for that."

"We'd have to have sex for that."

"Which isn't happening," I say, feeling prickly from the conversation about lingerie. And porn. "Not because I'm a virgin, though. I've had sex before."

He does this soundless laugh. "Good to know."

"You're mocking me."

"You're a thirty-three-year-old woman. Of course you've had sex. Lots of sex. I'm not one of those uptight assholes who can't stand to be compared to other men."

"*Lots* is a little much."

"But don't worry. I'm not afraid of competition. When you scream my name it won't be because I was first. It will be because I was best."

Heat kindles between my legs, which is strange, because I don't like cocky bastards. Or maybe I do. The man I loved before wasn't exactly humble. I'd been so dazzled by him in the beginning. His interest in me felt special, as if we shared something.

He looked at me like I was the only woman in the world.

It was only later that I realized he could give

that look to many women.

He was a charming man. A seducer. A much older version of Finn. Which is the reason this fake relationship doesn't have a chance of working for real, even if we wanted it to. Men like that have no reason not to stray. Not when every woman is willing.

Of course there was a dark side to Lane.

He turned possessive toward the end. He called it love, though I'm not sure if he even believed that. There was an obsessive tinge, though. He followed me to college when I tried to leave him. He only wanted to use me, but he ended up ensnaring us both.

CHAPTER EIGHT

Finn

I'VE IMAGINED HAVING sex with Eva Morelli plenty of times.

What man hasn't? She's a beautiful woman.

But I've never thought about who she does have sex with. Presumably she dates—real dates, not pretend dates. *I don't like charming men.* Even if she isn't interested in a relationship, presumably she has hookups, at least sometimes. Pretty much everyone single pairs up after those glamorous balls and galas. She might be too busy when she plans them for her parents or for her brothers, but she attends them, too.

There's always Tinder, though I can't imagine her showing up to swipe right or left. I can't imagine mere mortals having a chance with her. She's like a goddess. Like you'd visit her at a temple, arms full with priceless offerings.

"So who was the lucky guy?" I ask, being a nosy fucking bastard. "The one who took Eva Morelli's virginity. Someone from high school, maybe."

Even in the darkened car I can see her cheeks flush. "Does it matter?"

I have a feeling it does. There's an extra heaviness in the air. It makes me even more curious. There's never been gossip about her. Not that I can remember.

Never that casual conversation that haunts her siblings and cousins. *Did you hear? Sophia Morelli is dating a DJ who lives in Los Angeles. Tiernan is fucking a secret Constantine bastard. Selene was caught in the locker room of the 49ers with one of the players.*

No one in our circle can escape the gossip, but somehow Eva has.

Which means she either lives like a monk, or she's been with people who demand extreme discretion. Some politician, perhaps. Visiting royalty isn't out of the question.

"Come on," I say, coaxing. "You can trust me. I won't tell anyone."

"I know you won't tell anyone," she says, laughing a little. That dissipates some of the old grief in the air. "Because I'm not going to tell you anything."

She would need discretion if the person were married.

That would explain the absolute silence.

If the relationship continued, it would also explain why she wants this fake relationship.

I'm not judging Eva. I'm not even judging this random person, whoever they are. We're well past the times of Bridgerton, but in our social sphere, people still make marriages based on money and connections. That doesn't leave a lot of room for love.

"Where are we going?" she asks as I take a turn away from the Upper East Side restaurant I told her mother about. It's a very nice restaurant, the kind that Eva Morelli can go whenever she wants. She can go there whenever she wants, but it's not what she needs.

She needs excitement, like the underground casino.

She needs… Finn Hughes. Not the real Finn Hughes, buried under layers of secrets and grief. The surface-level version. The illusion of a charming, easygoing player. The man who can flirt with the mother and fuck the daughter in the same night.

I drive through Chinatown and over the Brooklyn Bridge.

Curiosity brightens her dark eyes.

Our destination is an abandoned warehouse park on Columbia. It's not somewhere she would have been before, with its rusted doors and broken concrete. Some of these buildings actually hold crates full of imports. Some of them deal drugs. One is a club that favors lo-fi music and opium. And this one? Well, it's arguably the worst one.

I park the car, and a man jogs over wearing a white polo shirt and black slacks. "Sir."

"Take good care of her," I say, handing over my keys. A couple hundred-dollar bills passed from me to him ensures my car won't get stolen or stripped while we're inside.

"Where are we?" Eva whispers.

Excitement tinges her voice, reminding me of other times she would sound this way. Breathy and curious. How she would feel underneath me, moaning my name. I force the idea away because there's also a note of fear. Probably because it sounds like there's a riot happening inside the building. The metal walls shiver in constant strain. The noise, and maybe even the bodies inside, push against it. They threaten collapse.

I take her hand. "Somewhere fun. You liked that last time. I thought we'd try it again."

"Are we going to play poker?"

"No, but we're going to gamble."

She glances around, where all other pads are dark. "My security would have a fit."

Not safe. You're not safe for her. "We can leave if you want to. I'm sure the hostess would give me a table if I showed up without a reservation. We went out a couple times six months ago."

Eva shakes her head, laughing. My words had loosened her anxiety, which is what I hoped they'd do. "So she'll give you a table with another woman? Are you really that good?"

Surprise races through me. Followed by lust. She clammed up when I asked who took her virginity. I thought she'd retreat completely, but here she is making innuendo. "Better, sweetheart."

"I'm almost tempted to watch you try."

"And I'm almost tempted to take you back to the car, spread you out on the goddamn sunroof, and lick your pussy so well you see stars. That way you'd know for damn sure how good I really am. But I promised I'd have you home by curfew, and if I start now I won't stop until morning."

She stares at me, lips parted in shock, eyes

dark with arousal.

Fuck, she's beautiful.

My cock throbs, but I force it down and nod at the bouncer. He opens the door, unleashing a whirl of sound and lights. We head inside to the bookie, a kid who's perhaps thirteen at most, with uneven complexion and shrewd eyes. At night he helps Old Max run the books. During the day, he ruins the curve in math for a New York State public school.

"Name," he says.

It doesn't matter that I've known the kid since he was four years old. Charles won the city's Mathathon, sponsored by a youth charity that the Hughes family supports. At the last charity picnic, he called me Uncle Finn. None of that matters here.

"Finn Galileo Hughes."

He writes it down.

"Galileo?" Eva asks, laughing.

"It's really my middle name." Though that's not why I said it. I said it to amuse her for the brief, glittering moment we share. It's like a bubble floating on the air. A perfect sphere that can only end one way—in destruction.

"Bet," Charles says.

I hand him a stack of hundred-dollar bills.

Nimble fingers fly through the bills, checking for more than the denominations. The texture, the weight, the ink. He can spot a fake better than a Fed. "Ten thousand," he says, confirming the amount. "Your pick?"

"Who do you think?" I ask Eva, pulling her close.

"I don't even know who's fighting."

I show her a picture on my phone, which shows two snarling, muscled fighters facing off. Matthew Thorn is the incumbent. Roth Wagner is the newcomer. "Come on, Eva. I have ten thousand dollars riding on your decision."

"This doesn't tell me anything," she cries. "They both look scary."

"What are the odds?" I ask Charles, who rattles them off without glancing at the screen.

"Seven point five to one, favoring Thorn."

"What'll it be, beautiful?"

"Are they really going to hurt each other?"

"It's a fight to the death, Eva. And the clock is ticking."

"Wagner," she says on a hard exhale.

Of course. It's very much like Eva Morelli to go for the underdog.

Does she even realize how rare that is? Especially for people from our sphere. We understand the privilege of money, how having some leads to having more. We understand the power of the incumbent. Eva knows it, too, but she has something else. She has hope.

Charles enters the bet and turns to the next person in line.

With a light touch at the small of her back, I point Eva toward the seats.

"I still have your quarter," she says. "From before."

"Keep it," I tell her, rubbing my hand over the small of her back. Even this small touch feels important to me, almost vital. "Double or nothing."

"They aren't really going to hurt each other, are they?"

"Maybe." Our relationship is fake, but when it's just the two of us? I'm going to be real with her. Honest with her. "Maybe not. But either way they chose to be in that ring. You don't stumble into it. You work your way there for years."

"Why?" she asks, sounding genuinely curious.

I shrug. "Some of them like to fight. Anger in physical form. Some of them are focused on power. A few look at it like an art form. Technique and form and even elegance."

"Is that why you come here? For the elegance?"

There's an open spot on the steel bleachers, and I guide her there. We're definitely well dressed for the event, but we're not the only ones in evening wear. We're not the only ones who ditched comfort for excitement. "I come here to entertain beautiful women."

"And that works for you, does it?"

"Absolutely. Something about watching two men beat each other into a pulp makes women hot. It's positively bloodthirsty."

"Don't get your hopes up that it'll work this time. I'm expecting to be horrified."

A cry goes up from the crowd as Thorn is introduced. He enters the room with all the swagger and pride of a born performer. The fact that he performs with his fists is beside the point. Another roar as Wagner enters the building. He looks fierce and determined.

He knows he's expected to lose tonight.

I don't make my living by throwing punches, but I know something about facing long odds. I know about hurtling toward pain and humiliation with no way to stop. You face it with your head held high, because that's all you have left.

"Thorn looks… mad."

He does look mad. Even more than the usual

posturing. I wonder if there's some personal beef between them. That doesn't bode well for that ten-thousand dollars. Thorn already has the advantage, and if he brings his A game, Wagner will go down.

The bell rings.

Nervousness races through her body. I feel it like electricity where I touch her skin. The first punch is thrown, and she burrows close to my body. I'm an opportunistic bastard, so I tuck her tight against my side, her soft breasts lush against my hard chest, her hair like sleek night.

The boxers dance around each other.

A punch. A dodge. They circle each other again.

They're learning each other, the same way Eva and I learn each other, our bodies in constant conversation. *Do you like that? Yes, more.* I stroke her hip with my thumb.

Thorn rushes in, secure in his past victories.

Wagner was clearly prepared and fights back with vicious precision.

The long, powerful exchange brings the entire warehouse to its feet. Even Eva jumps up, stepping onto the rattling metal bleacher in order to see over the tall men in front of us.

"Is he hurt?" she demands as Wagner staggers

back. He touches one knee to the ground, but he's standing again, back in fighting stance before Thorn can advance.

It's a solid match, but Thorn clearly has the advantage. He has more weight, more muscle, more experience. He's not as fast, but the blows he lands send Wagner reeling.

In a burst of speed, Wagner strikes, throwing Thorn against the ropes.

The crowd erupts.

"Yes," Eva shouts, jumping and clapping.

Her hesitation about the brutality evaporates in the face of excitement. She's one with the crowd now, cheering for her favorite, shouting encouragement when he's hit.

A one-two punch, and then Wagner is on the ground.

The ref steps in to start counting, but the fighter staggers to his feet. He's not looking steady, though. The fighters dance around each other, but it's clear one is fading.

Thorn pummels Wagner, relentless, stone-cold.

There's a reason he's the returning champion.

Eva tightens her grip on my arm so hard her knuckles turn white. "Finn?"

"Yeah?" I ask, my lips on her temple.

We have to be this close because it's loud in here. She won't hear me otherwise. And we have to be this close because she's clinging to me in both excitement and fear.

Mostly we have to be this close because it feels so damn good to hold her.

"You were joking about the fight to the death, right?" she asks.

"The ref will stop it if he goes too far." The word *ref* is a lofty term for what the man in the ring actually is. His only job is to keep them from killing each other.

And to count down at the end.

Wagner throws a hard jab, and Thorn's body recoils from impact.

Eva gasps. This is not a choreographed fight routine. This is not something for television. It's real. Fists crack against flesh. They tackle each other, use vicious holds that wouldn't be allowed in any of the real boxing matches.

She's shouting in the following moments.

I should be watching the fight, too. But I'm watching her. Surprise makes golden lights in her dark eyes. I feel the shock in the crowd. Then even more shouting.

"He's coming back," she says. Though I can only tell because I'm looking at her lips. The crowd consumes her voice. Something big is happening in the ring, but I don't care. I'm mesmerized by her excitement. It almost looks like arousal. This is how she'd be when I'm thrusting inside her, when she's begging me to go harder, faster, deeper. Then I'd change the angle. I'd press that spot inside her with my cock. I'd rub my thumb over her clit. Her head would fall back. Her eyes would close. Bliss would overtake that beautiful face.

Her shining gaze sweeps back to me. "He's coming back," she says again.

To hell with the boxing match.

A roar goes up around us. The bell clangs.

Someone has won the match, but I don't care who. I pull Eva close and kiss her. It starts off hard and demanding, a possessive press of lips. Ten thousand dollars is riding on that bet, but it's not more important than her. Not more important than this.

I lick at the seam of her lips, and she parts them with a surprised gasp. Did she think she was safe from me? Did she think she was safe as long as we were watching boxing or playing poker? I want her too badly for that. I deepen the kiss, and she responds with a sweet submission that makes me hard as stone.

Male calculation takes over. How quickly can I get inside her? Is there an empty closet somewhere in this warehouse? Can we make it to the car and park somewhere private?

A nip at her bottom lip is a promise—a promise unfulfilled.

She pulls back, her cheeks flushed with arousal, her eyes bright with surprise.

Her shock checks me. She didn't expect us to kiss, because we aren't really dating. This is a wild night out for a woman who specifically has no interest in relationships. That's why she needs to get her mom off her back. That's why she needs this fake relationship.

Desire leaks from her expression, replaced with slight embarrassment.

Eva Morelli doesn't kiss passionately in the middle of a crowd.

Except she did, with me. It makes me want to kiss her again, to prove the point.

Someone jostles her from the back. I catch her body securely against mine, but it's enough to shatter the moment. The shouts of the crowd pour over us. Wagner is doing a bloodied and bruised victory lap around the outside of the ring. While we were kissing, he won.

Chapter Nine

Eva

Adrenaline runs through my veins, making me feel shaky and overbright.

Adrenaline from the fight.

Adrenaline from the kiss.

Finn held me as if the world were ending, as if the cacophony that surrounded us was an apocalypse, as if that was our last chance.

It strikes me now, as I look at his hard-set profile, that he often acts like that. The underground casino, the secret boxing match. There's a desperate intensity to his actions, as if he knows there's a ticking clock counting down his time.

"Why do you come here?" I ask.

After crowding the bookie for their winnings, people jammed the valet and parking lot to get out of here. Rather than fight the rush, Finn led me for a walk away from the warehouses, down to the dark, gravel beach. If you had a boat and followed the coast long enough, you'd eventually reach the dock where he keeps his boats. There are no boats here, though. No yachts. No cute little seafood shanties and gift shops. This isn't precisely a good part of town. It isn't a safe part of town, but somehow I feel safe with Finn.

That's probably a mistake.

The intensity of the kiss proved there's something deeper inside him, a grief, maybe even an anger, that he keeps behind a thick screen of charm and playboy insouciance.

"Because it's a good time," he says lightly, but I can tell now it's a lie.

"It *is* a good time. In fact now I owe you fifty cents." But I'm coming to know him better. Spending time together, even in a fake relationship, is giving me insights into the man behind the quirked half-smile. "I think there's more to it than that, though. I think you seek out places like this, because you—"

His eyebrows raise. "Because I what?"

"Because you want to experience everything while you can." The words tumble out of me. My intuition is sure that's the case, though I don't know why he would be worried about time.

He's young, and more than that, he has the entire world in front of him.

"Is it because of work?" I ask, because I've heard rumors.

Everyone's heard the rumors.

He gives me a sideways glance. "What about work?"

"Your parents' expectations that you take over the company, that you perform, that you live up to the family name." I wave my hand to encompass everything. "I didn't have that pressure growing up, but I saw it in my brothers."

That earns me an indelicate snort.

"What?" I ask.

"You didn't have pressure growing up? The way I see it, you had the most pressure. You were the one everyone leaned on when they needed help. I'm guessing you were the one who woke up early to help the family and then stayed up late to help the family some more."

"It's not the same."

"Yeah, the difference is I get paid for my work."

I slide a little, my heels slippery over loose gravel. Finn holds me steady until we find better ground. "You know what this is? Deflection. You don't want to talk about your family, so you're bringing up my family."

He laughs, though it's a little taut. This isn't the charming, happy-go-lucky Finn Hughes that most of the world sees. This is someone carrying the weight of the world. "Fine. Yes, it's work. Yes, it's family. Yes, it's my parents' expectations. Happy?"

"Yes," I say, which doesn't make any sense. I'm not happy that he's hurting, but… "At least it's what you're really thinking. What you're really feeling."

He stops walking and turns to look at me. "Meaning what?"

"Meaning…" I can be outspoken sometimes. It's not a quality that men enjoy in women, or so my mother tells me. Which normally I don't give a fuck about. But Finn… the truth is, I want him to like me. Does that make me weak? Or does it simply make me human?

"Don't pull your punches now, Morelli," he says, faintly mocking.

I think of Wagner fighting against the odds in that warehouse. The cheers had been deafening, but I hadn't heard a thing once Finn kissed me. "This fake relationship? It's how you deal with the world. All those smiles and jokes and sports cars."

He puts a hand to his chest. "Leave the cars

out of this."

"There's so much more to you than that."

"How do you know?"

"Because I do."

He laughs in that soundless way he has. "That's wishful thinking, Morelli. I'm exactly as shallow as I seem. Not like you. You're so deep I could lose myself in you."

Why are you in a rush? I want to ask him. *Why does every kiss feel like the last one?* But that would expose me as much as him. That would reveal how desperately I want him to kiss me again. He sees it anyway. Even without me saying the words, he sees it.

He backs me up against a railing, and it doesn't feel altogether sturdy and typically hard. It's not a tame kiss. It's a filthy one. As filthy as that warehouse we were in. When Finn pulls back, he's breathing hard, only an inch away.

"I could lose myself in you," he says again, sounding uncharacteristically angry. "But I can't keep my hands off you. Is that fake?"

It doesn't feel fake at all. He tastes so good. He's kissing me too hard, almost, as if he knows that I can take it. And why couldn't I? I'm not a fragile girl. I'm a grown woman. I've seen what the world has to offer and lived to tell about it.

The way he kisses me now is not particularly careful. The way he touches me isn't careful, either. It's not the way he would have kissed me, polite and cautious, if he'd taken me to that restaurant.

This is wild like the fight, and I realize he's feeling an adrenaline rush, too. I thought he was used to those places. I thought it wouldn't have an effect on him, but his eyes sparkle with challenge. His eyes are also dark with other things he wants to do to me. He kisses down the side of my neck and returns to my mouth, like he can't bear to stay away. His hands move up under my dress. I have a fleeting moment of fear. If anyone sees me like this with my dress hitching up inch, by inch, by inch, then what? But who would see? No one from Bishop's Landing would ever come here. And if they did, they would just believe the lie of our relationship.

No one is here at all. There's no one to see us out here on this wharf, and so I let it happen. I know this is supposed to be fake. I know, I know, I know. But right now I only want to feel. And what I want to feel is Finn Hughes.

He touches me everywhere. His hands come up to the sides of my neck. They delve back beneath my dress. They skim down my hemline.

He groans when he reaches my breasts. He's as wild as those fighters in this moment. And it surprises me, exhilarates me. I feel just as much adrenaline now as I did when I realized Wagner was going to win. Finn is fighting now but I don't know whether he's fighting for me or fighting to hold himself back.

His hands go beneath my skirt, and I wonder if he'll do it. If he'll take me down to the dock and fuck me here in public in front of anyone who might walk by. It should embarrass me, it should make me recoil, it should make me push him away, insist that he stop, but I don't. I don't even think I would stop him if he took it that far. I think it might happen. That's how drunk I feel on him, how lost I feel on him.

That would be an escape. No one could deny it. Public sex. Where has this come from? What has this come to? I want everything.

"Maybe we could go…" I say, breathless. It turns into a moan when he finds my nipple. When he pinches it between two fingers. My head falls back in wordless pleasure.

I meant to say, *Go back to my place. Get a hotel room, any private space.* Because I want everything from him. I want everything with him, and we won't have time in public.

That seems to be a recurring theme with Finn.

Why is he running out of time?

His phone rings. I feel it before he notices. It's buzzing in his pocket. For a minute, he's still kissing me, his tongue hot on mine, his hands locked around the back of my neck. I'm grinding shamelessly against him when I feel that mechanical vibration.

"Finn," I gasp.

His whole body goes stiff. "Fuck," he mutters and reaches for his phone.

"Hughes," he says, his hand still on my neck.

A woman's voice comes over the line. I can't make out the words, but it sounds urgent. And I can see the tension cross his face. The excitement from the fight, the arousal from kissing me, goes out of his face. "I'll be right there," he says, and then he shoves it back into his pocket.

He tugs my dress back into place, his expression distracted.

"What's wrong?" I ask.

"Nothing," he says, but it's a blatant lie. We're back to pretending. "I have to get home."

"Can I help?"

He doesn't seem to hear the question as he tugs me back along the water's edge toward the warehouse. He still helps me over the loose gravel.

He's solicitous but efficient, and I sense the urgency in his actions. It makes a shiver run down my spine.

"Finn. What happened?" I ask when we're inside the car.

He looks at me as if he's remembering I'm here for the first time. "I'll get a cab for you," he says. Then he seems to realize that we're at this warehouse in a seedy part of town. "A limo. Fuck," he says again. "I'll take you back to my place. Then I'll send you home with our driver."

"Okay," I say, because I don't want him to worry about me.

Once he has a plan, he's all motion again. He's getting us into the car, pulling us out of the spot, steering us to the city at the very edge of the speed limit.

He runs a yellow light, then nearly misses a red.

Something's wrong. I can tell that from the set of his jaw, from the worried frantic look in his eyes. He shouldn't have to plan one more thing right now. Not a car, not sending me home. If something has happened with his dad, I can help. I can at least be there with him. Sometimes that's all you can do for another person.

"I'm going in the house with you," I say,

taking over.

It's what I've always done. If something's wrong, I help fix it. Like Finn said, I do it morning and night for my family. Which means I can help him now.

Finn gives me a bemused look. "No, you're not."

He's not sure of me. And why would he be? Our relationship is fake. I don't know anything about him other than his good family name. Other than he's fun at parties. Other than my mother likes him. "Let me help," I say, gently.

He shakes his head, but it's not really a refusal.

I recognize the look because I've seen it in my brother Leo. In my other brothers. Even my father. It's the look of a man stretched beyond his capability. Rare but made even more acute by how infrequently it happens.

No one can help. That's what the little shake of his head means.

He pulls his car past the front drive into a smaller, private area that leads into the back of the house. He turns the engine off with a jerk of his hand, leaving the keys in the ignition. I follow. He doesn't try to stop me. We rush toward the house.

"You shouldn't—" He cuts himself off.

"Don't worry about me," I tell him, squeezing his hand gently. He lifts his hand and looks at where it's linked in mine, as if surprised to find himself touching me.

Finn is worried. And there's a frantic energy coming from the house.

I let calm settle over me.

This is what I do for my family. It isn't always about running out of champagne in the middle of a party. Or even a possibly pregnant sister. No, sometimes it's been worse. There are dark things in my family's past. Violence. Pain. I helped my mother clean up broken glass from my father's rages. I found my brother at the darkest moment of both of our lives. The metallic taste of adrenaline floods my tongue. It's a comforting taste. A familiar taste. I learned early how to handle a scary situation. It's what I do best.

We step into a foyer that's beautiful but smaller, as if this is a separate residence than the main house. I don't have time to take in the spare, almost medical look of the space. My attention is captured by an older man in blue and white striped pajamas, barefoot, his brown hair standing up at the ends, a look of pure panic on his face.

"Stop," he yells. "Let me go. I'm calling the

police."

"Dad," Finn says, approaching him, his voice low but commanding.

Dad. The family resemblance wasn't immediately clear. His father's face is contorted in fury and fear, his hair a dark bronze instead of Finn's brown, his stature frail next to his son's vitality. Though now that I know I can see it in his eyes. His are more filmy, but they have the same shape as Finn's. The same shape as the eyes I looked into under the moonlight.

"They're holding me hostage," he says, his voice strained and vaguely hoarse.

"Okay," Finn says, sounding not particularly shocked. The resigned note makes it sound like he's heard this complaint before. "But shouldn't you be in bed right now?"

"I'm not tired," he says, sounding like a toddler who's missed his nap. "I want to go to work. Why can't I go to work? Bellows needs me. He claims he watches the markets, but he needs nudging. And that bastard Van Kempt needs to be watched. An eagle eye for property, but the mind of a gambler."

Awareness rushes over me like cold rain.

I didn't know what to make of Finn's father's claim that he was being held hostage. Was he ill?

Was it temporary? He didn't mean it literally, did he? Two harried women in blue scrubs stand back, present but allowing Finn to handle the situation.

It's clear this has played out in the Hughes home before.

Many times, probably.

I might still wonder, except I recognize the name Van Kempt. The man was a real estate tycoon before his untimely death this summer. He had worked his way up through the ranks at Hughes Industries before branching out on his own. I know this because where powerful men work is the topic of every ball and gala and masquerade that I attend.

He had his own company, Van Kempt Industries, for years.

And a well-known feud with the powerful Hughes family, to his detriment.

Why does Finn's father think Van Kempt will be at the office?

He wouldn't. Not unless he was still living in the past.

"I don't like the food," he says, a little calmer now. "They're always trying to feed me, and I don't want it. I want to go out. Sushi. Curry. Give me something with flavor."

"I'll order you some California rolls. Tomorrow."

"I want it now."

"Most places are closed. It's the middle of the night."

"No, it's not." Confusion passes over the older man's face. "The day just started."

Finn's mouth is a grim line. His voice is patient. "It's nighttime, Dad. You just woke up from a bad dream. We've gotta get you back in bed."

"I'm not going," he says, his chin in a stubborn lift. I recognize that movement, too. It's the same confidence that Finn displays when I challenge him. Though Finn usually backs it up with charm. His father looks like he's digging his heels in.

"Dad." Finn doesn't raise his voice. He doesn't seem annoyed.

No, he seems weary. The man who escorted me to an underground boxing match was full of life. This version of Finn looks like he's been tired for centuries.

"Mr. Hughes," I say in a quiet voice, stepping forward.

I don't know whether Finn will want me to say anything. Maybe he'd prefer I make myself scarce or pretend I wasn't seeing this, but it's not in my DNA. I have to try and help if I can. I don't know anything about the elder Hughes's condition, but I know something about defusing a tense situation.

He looks at me with a blank expression. "Who are you?"

I offer him a smile. "I'm Eva Morelli. A friend of your son's."

"Morelli," he mutters, his eyes growing vague as he searches his memory.

"I think you've met my father," I offer. "Bryant Morelli."

Awareness sharpens in those light brown eyes, and for a second I have a glimpse of how Daniel Hughes must have looked during his prime. "Yes, Bryant. A bastard through and through."

"Dad," Finn says, his voice sharp.

"Don't worry," I say with a small laugh. "Even he wouldn't deny it."

"Shame about that sister of his."

Sorrow washes over me. My aunt Gwen was the only girl with a bunch of competitive, arrogant brothers. They grew up strict Catholics, and when Gwen rebelled she was cast out. She ended up dying when I was very young. "I wish I'd gotten to meet her."

"You look like her," he says. "Beautiful."

The words make my chest feel tight. "Thank you."

He glances at Finn, then back at me. "Are you dating him?"

A note of tension runs through me. We're fake dating in a pretty public way. If this man had actually been at an office recently, if he had attended a society event, if he'd glanced at some of the gossip TikTokers, he would have already known we were together.

This situation is different. That much is clear.

Then again, wasn't tonight a real date? It felt real, even if it was only pretend.

"Yes, sir."

He grunts. "Good. About time that boy settled down."

"We aren't getting married, Dad." Finn's voice is still taut, but there's a note of humor underneath. An inside joke. A hint of the playful Finn I know well.

"Well, why the hell not? She's got good child-bearing hips."

My cheeks flame. "I'm not interested in marriage, Mr. Hughes."

He studies me. "Had your heart broken, hmm?"

"Dad."

"What? I know a thing or two about heartbreak."

"There are other reasons not to get married."

"Everyone wants love. It's the one human constant." Shrewd eyes study me. "No, you haven't had your heart broken. You've had it shattered. That's why you aren't interested in marrying Finn, even though he's a handsome, strapping young man."

I fail to repress a smile.

"Okay, Dad. We're really going back to bed now."

Rather than arguing again, the elder Mr. Hughes allows himself to be led down the hallway, one of his nurses in tow. I can hear him speaking to his son. "Don't let this one get away, Phineas. She's better than a rascal like you deserves. Better put a ring on her finger. Soon."

I watch them go, my smile fading, a bittersweet knot in my stomach.

Daniel Hughes has been the head of the large extended family for years. He's also the CEO of Hughes Industries. He's responsible for billions of dollars and the livelihood of thousands of people. But he isn't going into the office. It doesn't look like he can.

Which means someone else is acting as the CEO.

I'm guessing that someone is Finn Hughes. The carefree playboy act is just that… an act. He's the one handling everything, managing an international corporation and an apparently sick father without anyone even knowing.

Chapter Ten

Finn

"Phineas," Dad says, stopping in the hallway.

An oriental rug follows the long hallway, down many doors.

"What is it?" I ask, still bemused by the conversation that took place in the foyer. *No, you haven't had your heart broken. You've had it shattered.* Is it true? She hadn't denied it.

"Which one is mine?"

The question snaps me back to reality. A reality where my father can't remember which room is his bedroom, the same place he's slept for the past forty years. "At the end," I say gently, leading him by the elbow toward the apartment that's his.

"You really should marry that girl," my father

says.

"I know, Dad." It's easier not to argue. Not about the time of day. Not about whether he sends emails at the office. Not even about whether I'll marry Eva Morelli. That will never happen. Not only because she's had her heart shattered.

"It's time to do your duty. We need a Hughes child to man the ship."

That's the reason I won't ever marry. Because no one deserves to be shackled with knowledge of their own doom. I won't have children ever. The Hughes curse, as my mother calls it, ends with me. "I know, Dad."

I help him back into bed, and the nurse gives me a grateful smile as she sits back down in the corner. He needs constant supervision due to his tendency to wander. I nod back my gratitude, for handling my father's nightmare until I could get home.

My father grasps my wrist, hard, capturing my attention. "I'm serious. There's not much time. Look at you. You'll start forgetting things soon. It takes you quickly after that. Better do it while you can."

I don't blame my parents for their choices, but they aren't mine. "Don't worry, Dad. Everything will be fine. You just get some sleep.

You want to be fresh tomorrow."

"I have a meeting, bright and early. Board meeting."

"Okay," I say, though there's no board meeting. Only a breakfast of oatmeal with special vitamins added, since he usually doesn't eat enough. Bland food, the doctors insist. Spicy food interferes with his digestion. It gives him a stomachache, but when he's hurting, he doesn't know why. There's no cause and effect in his mind. The meal is long forgotten. So I have to make these decisions for him. The doctors explained that to me in calm terms, as if they were discussing the diet of my horses rather than my father.

One of these days I'm going to bring home an entire feast of curry.

Outside his room I stop and take a deep breath. Close my eyes. Count to twenty.

Christ. What a mess.

I return back to the foyer, but it's empty. Heading deeper into the house, I pass open doors leading to the drawing room, the formal living room. And finally find her in my father's office, sitting behind the desk.

Apparently we're going to talk about it.

Which means I need a drink.

I head over to my father's sideboard and pour a drink—because I'm a gentleman, one for the lady and one for myself. Three fingers. Then I cross the room and slide hers over. "Scotch neat," I tell her, before throwing mine back in a long, hard swallow.

She takes a sip and then coughs. "It's strong."

"It's forty years old. And brewed by distant relatives of the Hughes, I'm told. They have a distillery in the Outer Hebrides. Fifty percent of their sales come from Crown Hotels," I say, referring to a large chain of luxury hotels that spans the globe.

I'm not sure why I point that out.

Except I do know why.

So that she'll understand the importance of keeping this secret.

She draws her finger around the slender ring of the glass. It draws my gaze, because I'm a man. I want that finger stroking down my chest. I want it touching my cock. Her eyes are dark and fathomless. *Everyone wants love. It's the one human constant.*

Silence. She's patient. I'm learning that about her.

"Less than thirty people in the world know about it," I say, propping my hip on the desk.

Might as well face a problem head-on. "Half of those people are family. The other half are under strict nondisclosure agreements that would bankrupt them if they broke it."

"How?" she asks, sounding faintly impressed.

It's a good question. "Have you ever heard of the Hughes curse?"

"I thought that was an old wives' tale. And I thought it was about—"

"Their marriages." He gives a rough laugh, a sound of acceptance. "People sense that something's wrong, but they assume that because the business keeps running, keeps profiting, keeps growing, that it's only about their family life."

"Because *you* keep it running."

So she's figured that part out already. This is the problem with smart women. "Early onset dementia. Devastating for anyone, really. But when there's billions of dollars on the line? It becomes one of the best guarded secrets in the world."

"Why keep it a secret? If people knew you were running the company, they would trust you. Considering your quarterly stock market report, business is booming."

"You've been reading my quarterly reports?"

"I am a stockholder," she says. "And I think

they would trust you."

"They would trust me, but for how long? They trusted my father, too. How would they know when my mind starts to go? How would they know what I'm forgetting as I sign billion-dollar contracts? I would be thrown out tomorrow, and that's when the chaos would start."

She's quiet, and I know she's seeing it. The distrust, the factions, the fear—they're massive. Many levels deep. They would explode if everyone knew. "Do you have it?" she asks, her voice matter of fact, as if she knows I couldn't have accepted pity.

"Not yet."

"Then how do you know you're going to get it?"

"The main Hughes branch has only had sons for the past five generations. And every single one of us has the curse. That's what we call it, even in the house."

"If it got out—"

"It wouldn't be us who suffered. We have enough money stashed away to last lifetimes. It's everyone around us who would be hurt. They'd lose everything. Most of their money isn't liquid. It's stocks. Real estate. The value would plummet if we lost trust. We have tens of thousands of employees who depend on Hughes Industries for their paychecks."

"So… what? You're expected to sacrifice your life for them?"

She sounds indignant on my behalf. It makes me smile, which is a rare thing when it comes to this topic. "It's not such a great sacrifice. You've seen my cars. I have a good life. One many men would trade for. I understand my privilege. Just as I understand that I only have it for a few more years. Then everything—the memories, the knowledge—will fade away."

"Finn."

"Don't feel sorry for me, Eva."

"Excuse me if I don't believe in generational curses and old wives' tales. Maybe you'll get it, but it's not a guarantee. This is why you're like that, isn't it?"

"Like what?" I ask, wariness tightening my stomach.

"Like you need to live and laugh and… and *kiss* me, because there's no tomorrow."

"There *is* no tomorrow. I don't say that for your pity. I don't even feel anything about it. I've known it since I was old enough to talk. My dad isn't even fifty, but he's been gone for a long time. I have maybe a decade left before it starts, if I'm lucky."

"And then what? Are you going to train another generation of little Hughes sons?"

"Don't start. My dad is bad enough."

"Then why—"

"Because I promised him. I promised him when I was seven years old that I would take over Hughes Industries. That I would keep his condition a secret, no matter what the cost. No matter how he might argue with me later. And the peace I felt in him after that promise… it was real, Eva. He believed me, so I have to do this."

A pause. "I understand."

Of course Eva Morelli understands about family obligations. "But I sure as hell don't have to continue the cycle. My father didn't teach me dominoes. He spent our time together showing me all the companies, all the industries that would fall if Hughes Industry faltered. He didn't teach me chess. He taught me international contract law. He didn't play baseball with me. He taught me how to forge his signature."

Her eyes darken, and I know she's finally understanding how deep this secret lies.

"My brother will take over. He already has the Power of Attorney documents to all of our properties, our bank accounts, our corporations.

He can take over as soon as I show the first signs, whether I agree or not. And after that… after that, Eva, it's in God's hands."

"Because you're not having children."

I hesitate. This is one of the reasons my relationship with Eva can never be more than pretend. She comes from a large family. She may say she doesn't want marriage, but I heard the way she talked about children with her mother. If she does marry, I think she'll want kids. I can never give her that. I could never have children, because I would love them. And how can you sentence people you love to a lifetime of fear? How can you make them promise to lock you up, to tie you down—anything if it means keeping your secret?

They would watch me deteriorate before their eyes.

I'd be saddling them with more than the curse. I'd be saddling them with my care.

"When he was thirty-six years old he had his first episode. He drove to one of the Hughes offices in Queens and started ranting because he didn't recognize anyone there. They had to call the cops. We hushed everything up. People were happy to believe he was an angry drunk. They expect that of rich men, anyway. It was safer to believe that than realize he wasn't really there."

Her eyes are dark with sorrow. "God, Finn."

"I was sixteen. After driving him home, I pulled out my set of Power of Attorney documents and used them ever since. That's what he asked me to do."

"He had no idea what it would cost you."

"Christ, Eva. My suit costs two thousand dollars. My shoes another three."

"You're rich. I get it. It's not only money that makes a life worth living, Finn. Did he know how much it would hurt you to hide him away? To maintain separate lives? To split yourself into two halves so he could save his pride?"

She stands, revealing her curvy body in that incredible wrap dress. She made me hard when I first saw her, which was awkward with her mother and sister standing there. *She's got good childbearing hips.* I don't know anything about that, but I do know I want to hold her hips while she rides me, guiding her into the right rhythm, watching her breasts move, seeing ecstasy on her face. She circles the desk so she's facing me, and I set down the drink.

Nothing separates us but a few inches and a handful of luxury fabrics.

Oh, and the weight of both our family obligations.

She stands close enough that I can see the gold flecks in her dark eyes. I'm not sure what she's going to do. Call a cab and leave? Announce the Hughes family secret on national news? She wouldn't sell the secret for money, but she might do it as a public service announcement, if she believed that it should be shared.

Then again, she might do none of that.

She might strip.

I'm really hoping she strips.

Instead she leans close. Her arms slide around me. Her head rests on my chest. The pressure feels indescribable. It's like sexual pleasure but a million times more acute. A hug. That's what she's giving me right now. A goddamn hug. I've had sex, of course. Meaningless, physical sex with all kinds of filthy acts, but not this.

When's the last time anyone hugged me?

I can't even remember.

Chapter Eleven

Eva

My heart squeezes for how alone he's been.

Nothing is more isolating than a secret. I know that from experience, but at least I shared my shame with my brother. We took care of each other, Leo and me. He knows about my pain. I know about his. It created a deeper bond between siblings.

"Where is your brother?"

"Hemingway is at boarding school. It's easier that way."

"Easier for who?"

"He likes it there. They play lacrosse and eat ratatouille for lunch."

I smile at the description of what I'm sure is a very expensive boarding school. Lisbetta graduated from a girls-only version, Worthington Academy, this spring. "Where's your mother?"

Finn looks away. "She's in Vail," he says after a long moment.

"She's skiing?"

"I doubt it. But she enjoys the view."

"She's separated from your father, then?"

He gives me a hard look. "They had an arranged marriage. My mother knew the details of the curse before they married. They married for the usual reasons. Money. Security. Children. It was my father's unfortunate luck that he fell in love with his wife."

My stomach turns. "No."

"She had... some affection for him, maybe. Not love. It didn't matter. There's no way you can have a marriage with someone who can't remember who you are."

"He misses her."

"She stayed after the first episode. And the second. And the third. The decline started slow and then hit him like a freight train. The last time she saw him, he was ranting about the temperature of his paella. He was eating cereal. He threw it across the kitchen. Rare marble was covered in soggy Fruit Loops. Milk splashed on her Dior pantsuit. It was too much for her. Now she travels to our many properties. Some outside the country. Some in New York City. But never here in Bishop's Landing. She hasn't stepped foot on this estate for over a decade."

Bile rises in my throat. "What about your brother? What about *you*?"

"I'm an adult now."

My relationship with Sarah Morelli is complicated, but we're still close. I can't imagine only seeing my mother when we arrange a lunch date. The Morelli family, for all its many flaws, is apparently tighter knit than Finn's. "And your brother?"

"He visits her sometimes. I do, too."

He stiffened when I first hugged him, as if maybe he didn't want my touch. Didn't want my comfort. But after a moment of frozen shock, his arms circled me. They rest casually around my shoulders. His thumb brushes the small of my back. It's a small gesture that I'm not even sure he's aware of. Whenever we're touching, even if it's innocent, he's caressing me.

There's still tension in his body.

He's waiting for me to judge him. To condemn him.

To leave him the same way his mother left his father. That certainty lies in his bones. I can feel it in the loose clasp he has on me, the almost wistful way he looks into my eyes. Every second with Finn has felt like the sweetest goodbye.

There's a knot in my throat. Uncertainty.

Whatever I say next matters to this man. The carefree facade has dropped. Whether it will be there tomorrow morning, I don't know. In this moment it's gone. I can see the real Finn Hughes—a strong, loyal man. A man who's hurting.

He's grieving the ongoing loss of his father.

He's grieving the loss of his own identity and memories.

My father would probably say something about God's will. My mother would think the temporary pleasures were worth the long-term pain. And Leo? He'd probably believe in the curse wholeheartedly. It has the ring of punishment that works for him.

"You're a good man," I tell him, reaching up to kiss him on the cheek.

Surprise crosses his expression before he masks it in that carefree insouciance. "Is this your version of *it's not you, it's me?*"

"I'm not going anywhere. You're stuck with this fake girlfriend."

Amusement lightens those hazel eyes. "Is that

so?"

"Listen, I know you told me your deep, dark secret, but honestly? You're going to have to work harder than that if you want to horrify me. I've lived too long in the upper crust. Every family has secrets."

Something flashes in his eyes. Recognition. "Like your father?"

Shame heats my cheeks.

He came upon us at a party once. Intervened, actually.

Finn saw my father's hand around my wrist. He saw the crushing grip he used. It left a bruise the next day. Not the first one, which I'm sure Finn realized, the same way I recognized the frequency of the scene in his foyer.

My father is a powerful man. A smart man. And fundamentally, a broken man. Most of the world never sees that part of him. In public he's by turns cruel and charismatic. At home he's strict. He only gets violent when he drinks.

I know it's not my fault that he does that. Intellectually, I know. But the psychology of kids who've been hit is encoded early on in our lives. It doesn't flip when we turn eighteen.

My father isn't allowed to hurt me anymore.

I grew up, moved out, and stood up for myself. That too-firm grip at the party is rare these days, but it still felt more familiar to me than a kiss. I'm used to violence. Not love. Even in my romantic life, I'm used to betrayal. Not devotion.

"It's not exactly a secret," I say, because many people know. Even more suspect. Like Finn said about his father's breakdown in Queens, people expect wealthy, powerful men to be borderline alcoholic and moderately abusive. It's part of their privilege.

A sigh warms the top of my head. "I'm supposed to ask you to sign a Nondisclosure Agreement. I have a lawyer on speed dial for just such an occasion. There's a lot of money in it for you, I should tell you. Don't accept the first offer."

"Unfortunately for your family lawyers, I'm a wealthy woman."

"That usually doesn't stop people from wanting more money."

That makes me laugh. "I'll sign your papers for free, Phineas Galileo Hughes."

He leans back. "I should never have said it in front of you."

"Your middle name? I already knew it."

Brown eyebrows rise in question.

"The quarterly investor's reports," I remind

him. They're signed with his full name. As the Chief Financial Officer, it's not strange for Finn to write the reports. He's in the perfect position to know about the financial health of the corporation. And they assume that since his father's still the CEO, the directives and vision for the company come from him.

Now, of course, I know that isn't true.

Finn studies me so closely that it makes me feel exposed. "I know you're wealthy. And strong. And independent. But I'd like to help you if your father is still hurting you. It was never okay, not even once. I'd like to kick his ass if you'll let me."

What a strange idea, having this man at my command.

Like I'm a princess, and he's a knight that I can send on a quest.

"I had a privileged childhood," I said. "The best of everything."

"Not the best dad."

"No," I say softly, unable to refute the fact. "I'm not sure he'd deny that, either."

"I'd like to kill him for sure," he says, and it sounds strangely almost romantic. That's the last coherent thought I have before he leans close. His lips brush mine.

It's not the same wild, desperate kiss that we

shared before.

As soon as our lips touch, a sigh escapes me. This moment is a connection we never could have had on that dark, rocky waterfront. Not with all the secrets between us. The walls have come down now. In a temporary truce, there are no defenses. Nothing hiding the dark pleasure in his eyes when he pauses to look at me. Nothing stopping my surrender when he leans down to nip at my bottom lip. I moan both the pleasure and pain.

I let myself be open with a man only once. Trusting with a man only once.

It brought devastation to me. I promised myself never to do it again. What the hell am I supposed to do with this trust I feel for Finn? I don't like it, but I'm powerless to resist. *Powerless like you were before,* a voice in my head reminds me. *Blinded by love.*

Except I'm not in love with Finn Hughes.

That's the difference. That's why I can turn the kiss around, become the aggressor, nip his bottom lip and revel in the pleased groan he releases. His hands tighten on my body, pulling me close. I'm a curvy woman. Not particularly slender. He makes me feel like I'm delicate. His hands roam my body with hunger and more than a little awe.

"You're fucking beautiful," he murmurs against my lips.

The words strike a chord inside me, like a pluck of the piano's secret strings. I've been a help to my parents. A caregiver for my younger siblings. A friend to Leo.

But it's been so long since I've been a lover to anyone.

Long enough that it feels new when he rubs me against his erection. The hard length presses into my stomach, and I gasp. My thighs press together, instinctive and seeking. It feels bigger than I remember a cock being, but then again, I only ever saw one.

He flips our positions, so that I'm the one leaning against the desk.

This way he towers over me. Strong hands set my hips onto the desk. Papers flutter to the ground around us. Nondisclosure agreements, probably. Power of Attorney documents. There must be a million paperwork remnants of their family curse.

Neither of us care about that in the moment.

Now I understand why he's so desperate to experience everything.

I feel the same urgency when I spread my legs. It pulls the silk of my dress higher up my thighs.

He glances down at me and groans. The fabric of my panties matches the dress. "It should be illegal, how incredible you look."

A pleased blush steals over me. It's nice to drive a man like this, someone experienced, someone almost jaded, to this kind of desperation. But it's not enough. As long as he has words to charm me, I'm still not seeing the real him. The true Finn.

His caress steals up my bare thigh and around my hip. Along the sides of my body, almost ticklish if I weren't already shaking with anticipation. Then his large palm cups my breast, and I let out a shaky breath. He holds the weight in his hand. His thumb brushes the tip. My nipple hardens through the fabric of the dress and my lace bra.

"Eva."

I'm in such a dreamy state, I can barely focus. He has to say my name again before I force myself to concentrate. Of course he doesn't make it easy. He still molds his hand to my breast, warm and sure and possessive. "What's wrong?" I ask, my voice hazy.

"Did someone break your heart?"

I stiffen, but it doesn't do anything to dampen my arousal. "*Finn.*"

"I don't want to hurt you."

A fist around my heart. That's why he's hesitating. My heart might already have been broken once. He doesn't want to risk it. Specifically, he doesn't want me to get the wrong idea about this encounter. He might kiss me and touch me. He might even fuck me, but it's not going to change our relationship from fake to real. "You can't hurt me."

It's a lie, but he doesn't realize it. Or he can't wait any longer.

He pulls the dress down, along with the lace, revealing my bare breast. My skin looks very pale in the dim light of the office, my nipple a dark red. "Someone should lock you up," he mutters, still talking about how I'm illegal. It makes me smile, even in the midst of hurricane level passion, that he sounds almost annoyed that I'm sexy.

He presses a trail of feather-light kisses across my jaw. Down my neck. Across the cushion of my breast. His lips close over my nipple, and I suck in a breath at the heat. Arousal arcs through my body. It centers at my clit.

I want him inside me.

No, that would be too intimate.

My body doesn't care. It wants everything.

I lean in and kiss the side of his neck.

He shudders as if it's been a long time since anyone kissed him this way. Maybe it has. Maybe all the lovers he has in the city, and in all those fight clubs and in all those illegal poker rooms, haven't been enough. I want him and not just Finn, the man who smiled at a poker table, but Finn, the man who comforts his father, the one who's secretly running an empire, the one who hasn't said a word to anyone except for nurses and doctors.

And now I'm one of them. That's real enough.

I reach and fumble at his jacket. He helps me, shrugging it off. Then I go to work on the buttons of his dress shirt. My fingers feel useless under the onslaught of pleasure. He moves to my other breast, taking his time, tasting me as if I'm the finest wine.

I'm like the casino and the underground fight club, I realize. An experience he indulges in while he still can. He returns to my neck, and my head falls back. His mouth lingers on a place behind my ear, one that makes my breath catch. One that makes my thighs tighten around his lean hips. "Please," I whimper, though I'm not sure what I'm asking for.

The truth is that even though he's younger

than me, he has more experience. Exactly like he told me. The truth is that I've had my heart broken. The truth is that I'm terrified that it's going to happen again, and this time I'm not sure I would recover.

"Shh," he murmurs, soothing me, running his hands over my body. Maybe he sensed my sudden panic. "My sweet girl. Let me take care of you. I'll make you feel good."

I pluck at the thin fabric of his dress shirt. "Finn."

He yanks his shirt off, not bothering with the rest of the buttons. I hear them hit the desk and the wooden floor in small pings. An undershirt goes over his head.

Then he's bared to me.

I always knew that he was broad shouldered and tightly built. Part of me knew, in an abstract way, that he would look as beautiful without clothes as he does with them. But I had no idea. None. Muscles lay over each other in a masculine symphony. Springy hair covers a broad, strong chest.

God, I don't want to compare them. But I can't help it.

Lane Constantine was much older than me when we had our affair. I was only nineteen years old. He was forty-six at the time. He kept in shape, but his body was mature. Finn looks like a statue of a Greek god come to life.

I'm greedy for more. My hands run up his abs to his chest.

"I'm not going to tell anyone," I say, stroking muscles that are rock hard.

He grits his teeth. His nostrils flare. It's like stroking a bull, one who's holding completely still. "Good. Why are we talking about that right now?"

"Because I'm going to sign your NDA." I don't do it with a pen and paper. And I sure as hell don't accept hush money. No, I draw my name in large, languid swoops across his abs and chest. I use my full name, the way I usually sign. *Eva Honorata Morelli.*

"Fuck," he says.

Then I lean forward and lick one flat nipple.

He mutters his appreciation in a way I find too charming for words. "Lock you up and throw away the key. That's the only thing for you. You're going to start a riot."

Despite the heavy desire drenching my body, I find enough self-possession to give him a haughty look. There's power in making a man want you. "You're the only man here."

"You think I'm not going to walk all over this?" he says, the backs of his fingers brushing the insides of my thighs. Then he reaches my sex. He rubs the thin gusset of my panties, and I hiss out a breath. "You think I'm not going to wreck this?"

"I think you could try," I manage in a pert voice.

Challenge lights those hazel eyes. And pleasure. "Mouthy."

"You like it."

"I'm fucking dying for it," he says, dropping to kneel by the desk. My breath catches. Everything that happened years ago felt shocking to me. Illicit. Now I know that it was relatively tame. We never did this, for example. I'm nervous, suddenly. I don't know how I'll taste. I don't know if he'll like it. I don't know—

He pushes aside the silk of my panties. His mouth presses my pussy. His tongue does something slick and hot, and then my eyes are rolling to the back of my head. A keening sound escapes me. He finds my clit with unerring precision, and I jerk my knees together. It's too much. Too intimate. Too real. Strong hands hold my thighs apart, helpless for his invasion.

Then he slides his tongue in a circular motion. Suction makes my hips lift off the desk. I reach down to grasp his hair in my hands. I need something to ground me, to connect me to this man. I tighten my grip so he knows the sweet agony he's causing me.

He chuckles against my sensitive flesh. "Patience, sweetheart."

"Go to hell," I gasp out as he slides his tongue from bottom to top.

"Working on it," he murmured against my clit.

The vibration sends pleasure spiraling through my body.

There are papers beneath my head. They rasp against my hair, so thin and yet unmistakable. More documents, probably. Contracts. Obligations.

None of that matters right now.

He works my clit until I'm just about to come. And then he slows down at the crucial point. The first time I think he doesn't know. The second time, too. The third time I realize he's doing it on purpose.

"Bastard," I say on a low moan.

He stands, his expression hard with passion. I've never seen his handsome features so severe. I've never seen his eyes so dark. Hunger. That's what's making him this way. Need.

Two fingers slip inside me, and I rock my hips, begging and wordless.

Desire rises heavy in the air, but there's something else, too. Something sweet. Like the scent of honeysuckle on a humid summer night. The distant flicker of fireflies. A memory that's all too fleeting. That's how he makes me come, with his fingers inside me, his thumb on my clit, the moment slipping away no matter how hard I try to hold on.

Chapter Twelve

Finn

I'M ANSWERING AN email from the VP of Product when my secretary knocks. She stands at the door to my office, a stack of folders in her arms. There's an odd expression on her face.

"Yeah?" I say, still distracted by this earnings projection.

"Your brother's here."

My brother. I close the email. It's going to have to wait. "Send him in."

There's no point in wondering what happened. I know what this is about.

From the expression on Hemingway's face, my suspicions are correct. He's been kicked out of Pembroke Prep. Again. He strolls into the room, hands in his pockets. "Hey, big brother."

"Hem," I say, my voice even.

He drops into a chair across from my desk and kicks his feet into the opposite one. "Don't give me that look. The one that says: *I'm not angry, just disappointed.*"

My eyebrows rise. "Should I be angry?"

He grins. "Definitely not."

"Why don't you tell me what you did and I'll decide?"

He drops his head back, and from this weird angle I can see the resemblance to our father. I know I sounded bitter to Eva, bitching about my future. It's not mine that bothers me. It's my brother. My father was interested in raising me as his heir. My mother checked out after his symptoms grew intense. There weren't any parents left for Hemingway. I've had to step in, and I've done a fairly shitty job, considering he keeps getting expelled.

"Who was it this time?" I ask, resigned.

"I don't know why you assume I got into a fight with someone."

"Why *would* I assume that?"

"I mean, yes. I often get into fights, but that's not why I got expelled this time."

I give him a hard look and wait for the reason. He doesn't have any bruises on his face, which is odd. Usually, when they kick him out, he's got a black eye.

The other kid always gets worse, but they'll get in a few hits. I think partially, that's what Hemingway likes about it. Something real is happening to him, a physical sensation he can react to, instead of the hollow emptiness and distress. At least that's how I would feel about it.

He sighs. "I got caught doing something against the rules."

"Drugs?"

"Do we really have to talk about this?"

"Yes, we really do."

"It wasn't drugs. I was caught having sex in the bathroom."

Fuck. My stomach clenches. I should have had the sex talk. I'm late. I'm always too late. I scrub a hand over my face. "I'm failing you, Hemingway."

"No, you're not." He sounds indignant. "Me having sex had nothing to do with you."

Except it does. I should have known. I should have steered him away from this somehow. Physical fights only work for so long because you don't know about sex. And once you do, well, you open up a lot of other opportunities.

"Did you use protection?"

My brother rolls his eyes. "I'm seventeen years

old. That's like, basically ancient. Do you really want to sit here and explain the birds and the bees?"

"Did you use protection?" I demand, my gut turning to stone, because if he didn't, if he put someone else at risk, then it's on me. He's not even eighteen yet.

His brain isn't fully developed. It would be my fault.

He gives me a goading smile. "Why do you care?"

"Because it's important," I tell him. "You know why. When you have unprotected sex, you can get someone pregnant. Do you want to pass the curse to someone else?"

Hemingway looks away, his mouth twisted into a scowl.

He stares out my office window and his anger comes across the desk, his frustration. He came here directly from school. He's still wearing the uniform. They sent him straight to me, because where else would he go? Both of us are prisoners here. Not in the office, but in our own bodies. Our own minds. We both know how this will end.

We saw our grandfather decline in what was basically a private, luxurious prison. And we see what's happening to our father. That's what's lurking around the corner for us. Maybe I could have accepted it with grace if it had just been me. Knowing that it's going to happen to Hemingway, knowing that I can't do anything to stop it, fills me with hollow rage.

"There's no chance of him getting pregnant."

My brother's words hang in the air a second before they register. *Oh.*

I guess this is how my brother comes out to me. I weigh my words carefully, not wanting to fuck this up. Lord knows we have enough bullshit to deal with already. So I do what guys have done from the beginning of time. I turn something serious into a joke. "The bathroom? You couldn't wait until you were in your dorm room, like every other prep school kid?"

Hemingway snorts a laugh. "Fuck you."

The tension passes, and I let out a sigh of relief. Relatively painless, I suppose. For me, anyway. I'm glad there wasn't a risk of pregnancy, at least. "You should still use protection, you know."

"Oh my God."

"It's true."

"We covered this in health class."

Hell. I do need to have the sex talk with him,

but the corner office of Hughes Industries isn't the place for it. "I'll call the tutor," I say, resigned.

This is our standard procedure for when Hemingway has been kicked out.

A tutor will help him keep up with his academics so he doesn't fall behind. Hemingway studies like the serious student that he usually isn't. And when a few weeks have passed, I go back to Pembroke Prep and re-enroll him. Which mostly means that I promise he'll never do it again. The headmaster and I both know I'm lying.

Then I make a sizable donation to the school, and we're done.

It's always going to work out in our favor, right up until the moment it doesn't.

"Are you all right?" I ask my brother, my voice brisk. "Do you need anything? Are you hungry?" It can't have been a comfortable moment getting caught having sex in a school bathroom. There would be some adrenaline after that, some residual shakiness, even though Hemingway is playing it cool.

"I thought I would head home," he says, his voice hesitant. It's really a question, so he knows what to expect. Has dad had good days or bad days?

"He's getting worse," I say, my voice rough.

I don't want to admit it, but he'll find out soon anyway.

I remember Eva in my father's office. I remember her dark eyes looking up at me, her mouth on my skin. I remember the way I needed so badly to escape into her body.

Where is Hemingway supposed to escape?

With some kid from Pembroke Prep, apparently.

At first I drew lines in the sand. I thought this was the worst it could get. Then it got worse. I thought the nurses were bad. Then my father had a small stroke. He was unable to eat by himself for months. It was unrelated to the dementia but made it infinitely worse. He didn't understand the limitations. He fought them. That's when I understood the line in the sand kept getting redrawn. Feeding tubes and morphine drips and diapers. Everything is on the table. And dignity? That's long gone.

No one will see me like that, except for my brother. Definitely not some poor woman trapped in a loveless, arranged marriage. And sure as hell not Eva Morelli.

I want her to remember me the way I was in the office.

Even though I'll eventually forget.

Hemingway stands up. "Do you want me to make dinner?"

My brother is a surprisingly good cook. He could probably be a professional chef if he stopped getting into fights or fucking in bathrooms. "That depends. Are you going to make me Kraft cheese slices again?"

An eye roll. "They were yellow bell peppers, asshole."

This is how brothers bond with each other—by talking shit. He made some fancy dish that involved yellow bell peppers cut into insanely thin slices sitting in a tangy sauce. It tasted delicious but it looked rather like cheap cheese when arranged in a square.

"Then there was the caviar."

"Seaweed caviar."

"Seaweed caviar," I say, my nose crinkling as I remember. Unlike the yellow bell pepper dish, the seaweed caviar did not taste delicious. It tasted like... well, seaweed. My brother likes to experiment with food. Sometimes that works out great. Sometimes not so much.

"Am I seriously taking shit from a guy who burned spaghetti?" my brother asks an imaginary audience. He gestures to me, as if he were a lawyer in court. "He. Burned. Spaghetti. How do you even do that without actively trying?"

"It wasn't burned. It was just a little… dry."

"And brown."

"Only on the edges."

Hemingway stands up and stretches. "Whatever I make, you'll eat it and you'll like it."

"Nothing spicy."

His expression turns serious. "I know, Finn. Nothing spicy."

A million acknowledgments were in his eyes. It wasn't just about making bland food for our dad. It was about staying grounded. About remembering where we came from… and where we're going. Make food while you can. Fuck while you can. Get expelled while you can, because someday soon you may not even remember your own name.

I'm failing you, Hem.

Chapter Thirteen

Eva

Imagine a gladiator ring in ancient Rome. The weapons. The blood. The stray lion.

That is what a family dinner at the Morelli mansion is like.

You wouldn't think that charity foundations could have emergencies, but we got a call from an organization we've supported for years. They had a rare opportunity to get refugees out of a war-torn country, and we had to work quickly to vet their new efforts.

Nothing like transferring a few million dollars in a rush to get your blood pumping.

My phone vibrates. I glance down. A text from the organizer: *Wheels up.*

Relief floods my chest. I'd seen the manifest of high-value targets that were slated for evacuation, including women and children. At least they're safe. It feels like a drop in the bucket compared to the suffering in the world. And jarring as the limo pulls into the long drive.

Luxury pervades the grounds, even outside, where perfectly trimmed green topiaries rise from two-hundred-pound sculpted pots. The limo glides over the fine gravel. Not ordinary gravel. This was specially imported from Italy for its particular red-brown color.

There's always a duality to my work at the foundation.

I can make a big impact with our wealth, but no matter how much we give away, we live a privileged life. Right now children have only the clothes on their backs with them. We have a mansion with more rooms than we could ever use. I'm not sure I've even been in all of them.

The Morelli mansion has been in our family for generations. My great-grandfather purchased the land and built a more modest home. My grandfather tore it down and had the mansion built in its place, not sparing a penny on it. The facade looms large for any visitor, the large, dark front of it encompassing your view. It blocks out the very sun. Inside, every square inch has gold plating and hand-carved molding. Solid wood furniture creates comfortable nooks inside, leather armchairs with chess pieces. Expansive bookshelves with volumes in every language. A massive globe inlaid with ivory and diamonds.

My driver opens the door for me.

I take a deep breath and pause before stepping out. I am one of the gladiators, after all. And I'm late. I recognize Lucian and Tiernan's cars. Emerson's. The limo Sophia used to get here would be moved out of sight, just like this one will be. Leo's car is missing.

I speed dial him.

He picks up right away. "She's not feeling well."

He means Haley. Worry tightens my throat. "Do you need me to come over?"

"I already called the doctor. He swears she's fine. And I threatened him, so I'm pretty sure he's telling the truth. But that's why I couldn't make dinner."

"What's going on with her?"

"She had some strange pains and tension. She thought it was labor."

"It's too soon."

"I know." His voice is grim. A premature birth would be risky. Leo loves Haley to an extreme. If anything goes wrong, I don't know what would happen to my brother. Nothing good.

"You have to go to dinner, though. I need you to cover for me."

Which means I have to lie. If our parents knew there were issues they would descend with unwelcome help, my father with outdated advice, my mother with essential oils. "No problem," I say, my heart clenching. "Keep me updated."

He promises that he'll text me and hangs up.

One of the expansive front doors already stands open. A member of the staff holds it for me under the watchful eye of Trix, who's been the head housekeeper for years.

I nod a greeting to them both.

Her real name is Tricia Goodman, but Sophia nicknamed her Trix when she was a kid. She had a lisp and couldn't pronounce her name correctly. All the kids took to it. Only my mother continues to call her Tricia. And my father doesn't address her at all.

She manages the maids, the cooks, the groundspeople. There are Army commanders who could learn a thing or two from her strict leadership. There's never a speck of dust here. The decadent flower arrangements are always blooming.

No, only the people who live here are a mess.

There are multiple places to eat in the mansion. The staff kitchen, the family kitchen. The regular dining room. There's even a breakfast room. Our family dinners take place somewhere else—in the formal dining room, an expansive room that's more like a grand hall.

Despite the brocade chairs and heavy drapes, our voices echoed.

That was before.

Before Lucian married a Constantine. Before Leo found love. Before Tiernan stopped being so damn surly and surprised us all by settling down. Even Daphne fell in love with a reclusive art collector, though we're still keeping an eye on that guy. If he makes her cry, my brothers are going to twist his balls until they pop.

They'd have to get in line behind me.

Now there are way more people. Enough to fill the space with soft, teasing chatter instead of the stifling chill between my parents. Enough to make the room feel almost, *almost* loving.

Let's not go too far, though. We are Morellis, after all.

I wave hello to everyone, my brothers and their wives. Daphne and Emerson. Sophia's wearing a shiny silver dress with angles, her hair up in a high ponytail. The outfit would look silly on most people, but on her it's effortlessly cool. She pats a seat next to her, between her and my mom. It's the safety zone, but I give her a slight shake of my head. She rolls her eyes. Instead I cross the room, kissing cheeks and giving hugs as I go. I circle my father at the head of the table, giving him a kiss on the forehead before continuing.

I choose a seat in the middle of the table.

There's a reason I sit here instead of on either side with my parents. Because it's easiest to be the referee from here. As a bonus I get to sit with Lizzy and ask her about whether she's gotten her period. I tried texting, but she's given me radio silence since that morning.

I reach for the back of an empty chair, surprised when the dining room staff, a young man whose name is Mike, clears his throat. A faint blush tinges his cheeks.

He reaches for the one beside it. "Ms. Morelli?"

"That one's taken," Sophia says, her eyes twinkling.

I glance back in confusion. "By who?"

The only Morelli missing from the group is my brother, Carter. He's away on some geological expedition or whatever he does when he's not teaching at Oxford. He isn't due back in the United States until Daphne's wedding next month.

Sometimes my father will invite one of his friends.

Or my mother would invite someone intending to set me up.

My eyes narrow. If that's what happened, I'm not going to stand for it. I'm fake dating Finn Hughes for a reason. My mother should know better than to invite Alex Langley or whatever other older, plain, boring gentleman she wants me to marry.

"Hello, sweetheart." The voice comes from behind me.

I whirl and find Finn standing there. He looks impossibly handsome standing in the doorway in black slacks and a light blue shirt, the sleeves rolled up. His hair is just the slightest bit wrinkled. It's a different Finn than I saw at the underground fighting ring. And the handful of other dates we've been on: a Sunday morning farmer's market, Daphne's art show, and the Parkers' fiftieth anniversary ball. Different from the quiet, frustrated Finn I saw the night I met his father.

This is a domestic Finn, I realize. The one that comes home from work every day, a little tired but still with that irrepressible charm. His hazel eyes sparkle at me. It always feels like we share some secret, even though clearly I'm the one who's been left in the dark.

When I look back, my mother has stood to join us. "Darling, I knew you'd be pleased to have your boyfriend visit us. So I called him, and can you imagine? He was free."

He was probably *not* free.

No, he was probably coerced by my marriage-minded mother.

I'm sorry, I try to communicate with my eyes.

His gaze just reflects amusement at the situation. Of course he wouldn't show it if he had to leave work early for this. Actually, he's probably leaving his father's side. Guilt rises like bile in my throat. Or maybe he would have been with a woman. Or a man. Finn has liked both men and women forever.

I don't believe he'd lie to a woman, but he could have sex with her.

After all, we're only fake dating.

"Mom, he doesn't need to spend time with the family."

"Nonsense," she says. "He needs to eat anyway. And besides, your father and I want to spend time with your boyfriend. It's been so long since you were serious about anyone."

A flush burns my cheeks. *Please kill me.*

"Happy to be here," Finn says, smoothing everything over.

Usually that's my job.

I turn, almost blindly, and find the empty seat I'm supposed to use. That puts me next to Finn Hughes. In the center of the table, it feels like we're standing together in a spotlight. Sophia gives me a look that says she tried to warn me, but I didn't listen.

That's what I get for letting my defenses down in the gladiator ring.

"We don't have to wait for Leo," I say, because dinner won't start otherwise. There are two chairs on my mom's side waiting for him and Haley. "He had a meeting come up that he couldn't put off. He's going to be at the office until midnight, he said."

Concern crosses my sister Daphne's expression. She recognizes a lie.

My mother does not. She snaps her fingers to indicate that the servers can begin.

Several people in black slacks and white shirts come to pour wine and serve the appetizers, a high-end surf-and-turf offering with fresh lobster and Kobe beef seared in truffle oil. Clearly my mother spared no expense for this meal. The last time I saw her serve this particular dish, we had the Ambassador from Argentina at our table.

Apparently Finn Hughes ranks as high as foreign royalty.

"Sorry about this," I murmur once people start eating.

He pops a seared duck crostini in his mouth. "This is delicious. Invite me over anytime. Besides," he says, lowering his voice. "This is part of the show, right?"

Yes, it's part of the show.

The show where I'm fun and young and sexy enough to be Finn Hughes's girlfriend.

Not reality. Which would be funny if it weren't so sad.

"Part of the show," I murmur in agreement.

He leans close enough that I can see the deep green in his hazel eyes. "Besides, I wanted to come. I'm looking forward to seeing you in your natural element."

"It's not that interesting," I assure him.

"I doubt that."

I'm distracted from that cryptic comment when I hear Sophia's voice rising at the end of the table. Her expression tells me that Mom has been criticizing her again. My sister loves avant-garde art and nightclubs that serve fifty-dollar cocktails. It's harmless, really. But my mother acts like my sister is about to become a stripper for five-dollar tips.

"Mom," I say to distract her. "When did you invite Finn? You could have told me."

She waves her hand, and out of the corner of my eye, I see Sophia's expression of relief. "It was a last-minute thing," she says, lying through her teeth, because the next course is fatty tuna and caviar, which is probably two hundred dollars a plate. "You know I love seeing my children, but it's sad with Carter gone. I thought Finn could fill the empty place."

"Does anyone actually know where he's gone?" Daphne asks.

"The Republic of the Congo," Tiernan says in his low rumble.

"He mentioned something about Thailand," Elaine says, glancing at her husband, my brother Lucian. He shrugs, clearly more interested in gazing at his wife than speculating about his brother's whereabouts. He was possibly the meanest of all the Morellis, even including my father, before Elaine tamed him.

Lizzy snorts. "The last time I asked him where he was going I got a thirty-minute lecture about this endangered deciduous shrub that's only found in a particular five-hundred square miles in Siberia."

My father claps his hand on the table. "I don't know why my son has to go off chasing endangered panda bears when we have a company to run right here in New York City."

"It was a shrub," Lizzy says, somewhat mulish.

"Actually, panda bears aren't endangered anymore." My brother's wife, Bianca, wears an earnest expression. Her love for the environment comes up often. "There are over eighteen hundred of them living in the wild thanks to conservation programs in China."

"Carter is a professor at Oxford," Sophia says, scrolling on her phone, probably booking luxury villas in all the places we're mentioning. "Why does he get to have adventures? I thought they were supposed to wear tweed and have gray hair."

"Put your phone away at the table," my mother tells her.

"Didn't your aunt have a panda?" Emerson asks, his expression thoughtful.

Finn winces. "I was hoping no one remembered that."

"It made quite a stir in the rare collectibles community."

"Your aunt had a panda?" I ask, afraid to hear it will be a hide or something. I'm not passionate about the environment the way Bianca is, but I still don't like hunting for sport. Especially when it comes to not-quite-endangered species.

He sighs. "She was having a midlife crisis. She read something about this woman who captured the first baby panda and brought it to America. And decided to try it herself. I found out when an alt-PETA group decided to break into Hughes Industries at night to express their displeasure. It took forever to get the grass stains out of the upholstery."

"What happened to the baby panda?" Bianca demands to know.

"It was returned safely," he assures them.

Bianca still looks suspicious, but the conversation moves to Daphne's wedding, something that my mother never tires of talking about. My father is only interested in the guest list. He wants the most prestigious people to attend. Daphne is fighting for it to stay small, but it definitely runs the risk of turning into a circus.

Or a gladiator ring, as it were.

"How was it returned?" I ask, my voice low.

A soft laugh. "Yes, I had a baby panda in my Lamborghini. No, it didn't fit in the baby seat. Nor was it precisely a baby. It tried humping my leg while I was driving through New Jersey."

"Oh my God."

"I surrendered it at the Central Park Zoo, along with a very large check to keep the animal safe until it could be returned to its home in nature."

"It's official. Your family is actually more wild than mine."

"You didn't think it was possible, did you?"

Looking around at all the people I love, I huff a laugh. "No, not really."

Daphne's voice rises. She tries to assert herself, but she's a people-pleaser at heart. She's always struggled with disobeying our parents. Incipient tears thicken her voice. "I said we weren't inviting more than five hundred people."

My mother does her magic hand waving thing. "That was an estimate."

"It was a limit," Emerson says, his voice hard as steel. He's obsessed with my sister, which is a point in his favor. But he wouldn't hesitate to start a fight to defend her. Daphne is near tears, and this particular gladiator ring is about to draw blood if I don't stop it.

"Seems to me that since we're paying for this," my dad says, "we get to decide."

"We're paying for it," Emerson says, as if it's final.

No one tells my dad what to do. Especially not a man who maybe kidnapped my sister barely six months ago. Sure, he gave her back, but it still leaves him on thin ice. I've spent enough time at his modern beachfront home to get to know him. To trust him. Leo makes a point of having Emerson and Daphne over to his house for dinner on a regular basis for the same reason. But over the past six months, other members of my family have considered locking her up in the Morelli mansion until she recovers from Stockholm Syndrome.

"Dad," I say, my voice loud but calm. "Did you get my email about the foundation's upcoming gala? I need you to give the keynote address this year."

"Make Lucian do it," Sophia says. "He's the one who runs Morelli Holdings."

"Thanks for volunteering me," Lucian says.

The two siblings have a long-standing history of needling each other. Unfortunately, that also raises the tension in the room. After a power struggle at Morelli Holdings, my father lost his position as CEO to his oldest son. He's never really accepted it.

My father stands up, looking fierce. "We are giving you our daughter's hand in marriage," he says to Emerson LeBlanc. "One would think you might be grateful."

Emerson leans back, unbothered by my father's aggression. People may underestimate him because he's an art collector, but he had a hard childhood. It taught him to be strong in the face of bullies, even rich ones.

"You can't give me what's already mine," he says.

Shit.

I stand up and put my hands out. "Listen."

Even Tiernan looks pissed at Emerson now, which isn't a good sign. He had a falling out with my father, but the truth is, he can't so easily shed the position as his watchdog. And who knows what Lucian would do if a fight broke out. He'd be a wild card.

My father growls something that should not be repeated in polite company, and Emerson gets to his feet.

Daphne gives me a panicked look.

Fuck.

"I have an announcement to make," I say,

loud enough that the whole room stops to look at me. I take a deep breath, the same way I did before I exited the limo. This family is crazy and a little bit violent, but they're mine. "An important one."

And I have the next ten seconds to think of something.

There is no actual announcement. It's just that they were going to fight, and I'm the person who breaks up the fights. The person who stops them from happening. The person who diffuses a thousand different situations in my family. Which means I need to think of something big enough to distract them from punching each other about Daphne's wedding.

"We're engaged," Finn says, standing up, his hand going around my waist.

Stunned, I let him pull me close to his side.

My brothers look pissed. My dad looks genuinely shocked. My mother's about to swoon.

Silence lands in the dining room for a taut few seconds—*one, two, three*.

And then all hell breaks loose.

Chapter Fourteen

Finn

I FINALLY TAKE Eva to the fancy restaurant on the Upper East Side.

No illegal poker club. No underground boxing match. I did consider taking her to a drag race, but I decided to mix things up. Candlelight and Wagyu steak will keep her on her toes. The maître d' escorts us to the best seat in the house.

People glance at us on our way to our seats.

That's the reason why people come to this restaurant. The gourmet food and the Michelin-starred chef? They're like popcorn at a movie theater. Someone is probably tweeting about us right now. A blurry side shot of us walking will make its way onto TikTok.

That's what it means to be a Hughes dating a Morelli in New York City.

Of course we're not fake dating anymore.

We're fake engaged, which Eva is not happy about.

She barely said two words to me the rest of dinner. Her response to my invitation was pleasant but not particularly enthusiastic. I'm sure we'll talk about it.

A waiter comes over, all ingratiating solicitude.

Her expression is carefully blank as she examines the wine menu. "The 2016 Produttori del Barbaresco," she says, handing him the heavy leather-bound list.

"Scotch," I tell him. "Neat."

I don't usually drink it before dinner, but there's a cool reserve in Eva that makes me think I'm going to need it. There's at least a fifty-percent chance that she's going to tell me she's done. Done with playing pretend. Done with the fake dates. I know I shouldn't care. We mostly did it to get her mother off her back, though being spared some of my mother's prodding has been nice. She doesn't live in the country, most of the time, but she can still text plenty of mom guilt about my lack of progeny. I shouldn't care if Eva wants to stop fake dating me, but the thought of it makes lead sink in my stomach.

The waiter bows slightly and leaves us.

A tense minute follows.

"What the hell were you thinking?" she finally says.

"You're welcome," I say, mostly because I know it will annoy her. I don't know why I'd want to annoy her, except anything is better than that cool indifferent mask. And it *is* a mask. I know it is. We may be fake dating, but the connection between us isn't fake.

"You know my mother has calls out to a hundred wedding venues, right?"

Ouch. "We can say I want a long engagement."

"Florists. Cakes. The entire thing is already crazy for Daphne. My mother called me twenty times today before I got here, asking for my favorite winter colors."

"Tell her my father is withholding his approval on the match."

"So my father can get offended and show up at the Hughes estate? No, thank you."

"Listen, Eva. I'm sorry. I don't know why I said it. Well, yes, I do. I said it because you were trying so hard to protect Sophia from your mother and to protect Daphne from your father. And then you were trying to protect your father from Emerson." My voice must have risen, because someone from another table looks over at me. I'm not yelling, but I'm sure as hell not going to let Eva turn herself inside out trying to please her unpleasable family. "And I was tired of watching it happen. You're protecting everyone. Who's protecting you?"

She stares at me, her mouth open. I half expect her to slap me for calling her out like this. For calling her family out. She's nothing if not loyal to them.

Instead her dark eyes soften. "You were trying to protect me?"

Exasperation makes my laugh sharp. "Eva Honorata Morelli. You are the strongest, smartest, most beautiful woman I've ever met. And you let your family walk all over you. Grown men and women who can't last a single night without you coming in to save them. It makes me want to take you far away and chain you to a beach chair until you relax and forget about everyone else."

Her lips quirk. "You remember my middle name."

I laugh, though there's not much humor in it. "You don't want to talk about this."

"Yes, I do."

"You wrote your name across my chest with

your finger. I'm going to remember that night for the rest of my life." I shake my head. "No. Of course I won't. Someday I won't remember you at all, which is a goddamn shame. Your naked body is a work of art."

Sadness clouds her face, and I regret my words. It's just so strange to have someone who knows my secret. It made me relax. But of course, there's a reason it's a secret. Because it makes people uncomfortable. Eva is too sweet and pure to judge me for it, but the truth is, she doesn't like it any more than the rest of the world would.

It's called the Hughes curse for a reason. It's my cross to bear. Not hers.

She sighs. "You're right. Sometimes I do go a little too far trying to keep the peace."

I still remember the way her father gripped her arm at a party long ago, his anger thick in the room. They thought they were alone. The skin around his fingers had turned white. I interrupted them. "You did more than keep the peace. You were abused."

Something fierce flashes through her eyes. "That was one time."

I give her a look that calls bullshit. Loyalty is admirable, but I know the truth.

She looks away first. "Families are complicated. I thought you understood that."

"My relationship with both my parents is complicated, but I can tell you that neither of them has ever hurt me. Well, I suppose that's not strictly true. My father has been known to fight during his worst hours, but when he does that he's not in his right mind."

"My father wasn't in his right mind either," she says, her voice quiet.

Christ. She's enabling them. I can't blame her, because I've seen how intensely she loves them. It's in her nature to protect them, even if they don't deserve it.

The same way she protects you, a small voice says inside me.

I push that idea away. I'm not hurting her.

Aren't you?

The waiter comes back with our drinks and takes our order.

When he leaves we sit in a silence that's actually quite comfortable. She looks beautiful. That's what keeps distracting me. Everything about her is flawless. Everything about her is queen-like. We might be fake engaged, but if I were ever going to marry, if I had to choose someone, I would want someone like Eva. No, not someone like her. Just her. This specific, incredible woman who drives me insane with lust.

As I study her, I notice a faint sadness in her eyes.

"What's wrong?"

She gives me an arch look. "Nothing."

"Don't tempt me, sweetheart. If I have to coax the truth out of you in front of all these witnesses, I have no problem doing it."

Her cheeks turn pink. "I'm a little worried."

"About?"

"About Haley. She's pregnant, and she keeps having these false contractions. The doctors say it's normal, but my brother is so worried."

I reach across the table and take her hand. "Can I help?"

Her eyes meet mine. "You are helping, just by listening. I can't tell anyone else in the family, because they'd only worry. Or worse, descend on their house. Leo is always overprotective, but in his current state he'd probably get arrested."

"I'm sorry."

"I mean of course I'm worried about the baby. And Haley, who I really care about now. But I'm more worried about my brother. Leo has been through so much already. And he loves Haley beyond what can be healthy. If anything happens to her…"

I wait a moment, but she doesn't finish the sentence. "We don't have to stay here, sweetheart. I can take you home or to Leo's place or—"

"No," she says, a faint pleading note in her voice. "I want this. Need it. Show me what it would be like to have a real date with Finn Hughes."

"So the other dates weren't real?"

"They were," she says with a soft smile. "In a way they're the realest things I've ever done. But I like this too. Both sides of you."

"Dr. Jekyll and Mr. Hyde?"

"Maybe. If Dr. Jekyll were a billionaire who was too handsome for his own good. And if Mr. Hyde were secretly strong and grieving and lonely."

"I feel like that story wouldn't make a great musical."

"No," she says. "But it makes a great man."

Warmth suffuses my chest. Goddamn. This woman really should be illegal. Not only because she's sexy, but because she's the real deal. Not like me. I'm fake. Pretend. Temporary. Every second that I spend with her, I'm one step closer to the end.

Oh, everyone knows we're not promised a long and healthy life.

We can live with that uncertainty.

Unfortunately, my fate isn't uncertain. I know exactly how it's going to play out. And I watched my mother lose affection for my father as he drooled and babbled and essentially turned back into a child. I watched my father, in his lucid moments, ask for her.

I lie, of course. *She's shopping. She's at the spa.* Anything but the truth, which is that she hasn't been in this house for years. In a matter of hours he's forgotten about her again.

It's a strange blessing.

I raise my hand to call the waiter over. "Put a hold on the foie gras and the risotto. We're having dessert first. One of everything. And I expect at least one thing to be on fire."

She smiles, like I hoped she would.

Christ.

I could spend a lifetime with this woman.

The only problem is, I don't have a lifetime left to live.

"Tell me something about you," she says after eating a bite of chocolate cremeux and caramelized banana. "I know about the casino and the boxing. Do you spend all your time seeking out illegal activity or do you have other hobbies?"

"Horses," I tell her. "I breed them. Race

them."

A small notch forms between her eyes. "I remember seeing something about that. An article somewhere. That you were the youngest owner to win the Kentucky Derby."

"It's not precisely an achievement, owning them. It's the jockey that does the work. And mostly the horse. You don't make them race, you know. They want it. The real champions want to push the limits of what they can do, just like human athletes do."

"Ah," she says in a knowing tone.

"Ah, what?"

"It's another one of your risky things. Like gambling."

"There's definitely a gambling element to horse racing. And they've made me a lot of money. But the truth is, I feel a connection to the horses. An understanding."

"You like to be ridden?" A moment after the words are out, she turns pink.

I'm a gentleman enough to ignore it. Barely. "The horses are bred to be champions. They enjoy it, but they were also made that way. They can't help it."

She frowns. "Is that how you feel? That you were... bred?"

My voice drops. I'm aware that people are around us, even though they can't really hear. "I know I was bred. That's why my parents got married. Someone had to carry on the family name."

"You have the horses at your estate?"

"There's not enough room for them. We have a property upstate. I visit when I can, which never seems like enough. Especially now that Hemingway is home."

"Your brother?"

I make a face. "He got expelled."

"Oh no."

"He was having sex in the bathroom. I feel... pretty useless, actually. I should have had the birds and the bees talk with him years ago. And maybe a sexual orientation talk. And a gender identity talk, maybe. I don't even know. I'm failing him."

Sympathy crosses her face. "I feel the same way." Her voice drops. "Lizzy thought she might be pregnant. She took the test at my loft. Negative, thank God. She's supposed to start college in the fall. She has a lot to do before she's ready for kids."

I stare at her, surprised that I never put it together before. "We're the same."

"What?"

"You and I. Both of us are raising our siblings."

Awareness raises her brow. "You're right."

"Though you have quite a few more than I do."

No fucking wonder I was drawn to her. She's beautiful and perfect and… the same as me. We share an experience that's shaped us. That connection remains while we finish the dessert and finally get our entrées. Our conversation turns a little lighter, but it never becomes completely playful. There's a new gravity between us, pulling and pulling.

When we're done I help her stand and lead her out of the restaurant.

A man approaches me, his expression intent, and I force myself not to flinch. I try to offer a handshake, but he pulls me in for a hug. He's my father's friend. No, scratch that. He's my father's *best* friend, which makes it that much worse.

Which is why I've been very careful not to make close friends.

"How's Dan?" he asks, trying to mask his hurt and not being very competent at it. "I've missed him at the country club. Other guys ask me about him."

"He's fine," I say. "Private. You know how it is."

"Right. Right. When does he want to meet up for golf? You'll pass the message along, won't you? Tell him to give me a call. Or email."

"I'm sure he'll appreciate the invitation, but he's pretty busy lately."

A resigned smile. He thinks he did something to piss my father off. Or that maybe my father and him were never friends, that he just imagined it all. I know because I feel that way too, sometimes. When my father doesn't remember something, when he seems so sure that it's twenty years ago. It's a mindfuck, this disease. On my father and everyone else.

Chapter Fifteen

Eva

Finn's quiet when the valet brings his car around.

No wonder why. Those comments from his father's friend had to hurt.

Most people couldn't see it. His mask was firmly in place—the charm and the easy humor. But I saw underneath. Maybe once he dropped the mask, it left him a little vulnerable. Only to me, though. Even my own body tensed at the man's clear confusion. He didn't understand why his golf partner had disappeared, and nothing Finn said would fix that.

Except the truth.

Though I'm starting to understand why the Hughes family has kept their secret. I'm not sure the world really wants the truth. What would happen if he'd told that man that his father might not even remember how to play golf? He would get pity, at best. And suspicion, like he said, that he would fall prey to the same disease.

My family has other secrets. Worse secrets, really.

I have things I'll never tell Finn Hughes, which isn't fair. I know his darkest parts, but he doesn't know mine. It makes us uneven. It makes me a coward.

He pulls up in front of the building and gets out to open my door for me. I know what I should do. I should go upstairs. Leave him here. Let him get back to his family...

"Do you want to come upstairs?"

He nods, wordless.

He's quiet again on the way up and I realize this is different. This is different from when he came here before to get me for our date. Arousal simmers in the air. Anticipation as well. Are we going to have sex? That's what people do, right? When they invite a man upstairs after dinner? That's how dating works, I think. I wouldn't know, because I've barely ever dated. I've only had sex with one man, and that was done in furtive, secret meetings.

Having a man follow me up the stairs to my

loft is new.

And so I feel shy when I open the door to my home.

The walls are painted various jewel tones—navy blue and emerald green and aubergine. That was how my grandmother did it, each area themed to the space. Ornate antique furniture covers every inch of the walls, each surprising in its way. An antique TV has been hollowed out and now serves as a lighted liquor cabinet. Paintings and quilts cover the walls. Chandeliers hang from the high ceilings, along with a four-foot-tall stained-glass whale.

Ironically the strangeness of it all makes it feel safe and comfortable.

It's a place where the decor is so bizarre that you can feel free to be yourself. Nothing you do or say will be more strange than some of the pieces here. There's a pink lacquer statue of a dog next to a miniature library—classic books printed in one-inch volumes. A neon sign proclaiming *CIGARS & MARTINIS* was possibly stolen from some unsuspecting club years ago.

I moved in the second I turned eighteen. And sure, I could have changed the decoration. My mother practically begs me to do it every time she visits. I love it, though.

My main addition is the terrariums.

I probably should have warned him about those.

He might think it's weird. Well, that's because it *is* weird.

Like a magnet, he's drawn to one despite all the other things to look at. This one is small enough to hold in one hand, perfectly round, packed with moss and stones and a small porcelain figurine of a realistic-looking T-rex. In his tiny hand is the stem of a single orchid, which blooms white, reaching outside the round opening of the terrarium. It reminds me of the orchids at the gala for the Society for the Preservation of Orchids.

It's quirky and irreverent.

In other words, it fits into the vibe of the loft perfectly.

He glances back, his lips quirked. "You made this?"

"It's kind of a hobby."

Unerring, he wanders over to another one. This one's larger and themed more like a fairy garden, with a small cottage and a wooden bridge over a babbling brook made out of moss.

"That's reindeer lichen," I offer, babbling in my nervousness. Am I supposed to give him a tour? A coffee? I have no idea about the after-dinner customs. Or maybe I'm supposed to 'slip into something more comfortable' and come back in lingerie. It would help if I owned lingerie. "My brother Carter brought it back from northern Canada. He said it's green when it's fresh, but it turns blue when it's dry."

Somehow when he looks back at me, he's close. Close enough for me to feel the warmth of his body. Close enough to turn flushed under his intense regard.

"You're nervous," he murmurs. Not a question.

"No. Maybe."

He puts his hand on the side of my neck. His thumb brushes my pulse point. I can feel it, a little too fast. My breath sounds loud between us. "We don't have to do anything," he says. "We can just have a glass of wine. Or maybe I can leave, if you want me to."

He can leave. If I want him to. The meaning of words is slow to register. My mind feels weighted down with desire. Like I'm made of silk-thin petals, and the desire is dew. Do I want him to leave? That's the safest thing to do, for both of us. Do I want to talk and open a bottle of wine? Also safe, but that's not what I want. There are

Alex Langleys of the world if I want safety. I'm with *Finn Hughes,* the playboy billionaire. Other women would love to be with him, even if it was only for a night. This has nothing to do with other women.

Me.

I would love to be with him, only for a night.

"Stay," I say. "Make me forget."

Make me forget about Haley and Leo and their baby. Make me forget that I'm me and you're you. Make me forget that this is only pretend.

He drops his head but doesn't kiss me. His lips are inches from mine, but he doesn't take that last extra millimeter. He's waiting, I realize. For me to kiss him. He's too good to take me, if I might have doubts. If I might regret it later.

I'm sure I will regret it, but those regrets will keep me warm when he's gone.

I push up on my toes in my heels. My lips meet his in a clumsy, too-hard way. He doesn't seem to mind, kissing me back, pulling me closer. It's like I unleashed something inside him. That one atom of space—it was permission. Not only for sex but this other side of him. Raw and blunt, his tongue lapping my mouth with the same rhythm that he'd use to fuck me.

It's a promise. A warning.

When we were in his house, he licked me between my legs the same way. He fucked me with his tongue until I climaxed harder than I thought possible. I didn't even know my legs could shake like that. My time with Lane feels a million years away. I don't remember much about the orgasms, which probably says everything about them.

It hadn't really been about the sex for me. It had been love.

The opposite of this situation.

This has nothing to do with real emotion. It's only sexual pleasure. And I already know he can give me that. He deserves it, too. That night he didn't let me return the favor. Still shocked by the evening and disconcerted by the orgasm, I'd let him pack me into a limo with a driver and send me home.

That was his home. His domain.

This is mine.

I sink down to my knees and look up at him.

He sucks in a breath. "Eva. You don't have to do this."

Except he wants me to. The desire burns in his hazel eyes. And what's more, I want to do this. It makes me feel powerful, that I have something this man wants. He has everything, almost. This is a gift. I unbuckle his belt and open his pants. He lets me do it, not moving to help, only watching between slitted eyes.

I kiss the tip of his cock. It's slick against my lips. I feel unaccountably innocent right now, which is strange. I've done this before. But one man is not a large set of references. And I'd been young and foolish back then. Prettier, too. I don't think I'd ever had any real skill in this area. It had mostly been my enthusiasm he appreciated.

"Lick," Finn says, the green of his eyes turning deeper.

I obey him, licking around the head, tasting his desire. It's easy as long as he gives me commands. As long as he looks down at me like he's going to devour me. He stands tall and strong. It's a powerful position, him wearing a dress shirt and slacks, completely clothed except for the long, hard column of his cock. My thighs press together, seeking friction.

"How is it going to feel in your mouth?" he asks, stroking my temple. "Hot. Warm. Wet. I'm going to have to focus not to come down your throat."

My eyes burn with an emotion I can't name. Arousal is part of it, but there's more.

He continues, clearly not expecting me to talk

when I'm busy licking the underside of his cock. "You'd take it, wouldn't you? If I wanted to paint you with come. If I wanted you to swallow it down. You'd be a good girl for me, wouldn't you?"

I nod, wordless, overcome by sensation.

"Take me in your mouth," he says. "As far as you can go."

I lean forward to suck him deep. The large head hits the back of my throat, and I cough. My eyes water. My mascara might be running. It's embarrassing, really. I'm thirty-three years old. I should know how to suck a cock, shouldn't I?

He doesn't look disappointed, though. He looks like a king accepting the service he deserves. "Don't stop," he says. "Try again. You've got it. There's my good girl."

My sex throbs under his praise.

"Enough," he says, stopping me. His cock is still hard and slick when he pulls me to my feet. "I'm not coming in your mouth. Not before I get to feel your pussy."

The words make my breath catch. I want that, too.

Before I can register what's happening he lifts me in his arms.

He finds my bedroom and tips me onto the

bed.

Then he's on top of me. Almost feral.

"It's going to be more than once," he says, and I don't know what he's talking about at first. I'm too busy watching him. He drags himself away and strips off his clothes.

Holy shit, he's absolutely beautiful. He's beautiful in clothes, but without them he's stunning. It makes me lose my breath. I'm suddenly nervous, suddenly a little shy, but I can't bring myself to hide from him. I don't want to.

When he's naked, he positions himself between my thighs.

I hold my breath, wondering if he'll speak to me now. If he'll praise me like he did before. His eyes meet mine. And I understand that there will be no praise right now.

We're beyond that. Past words.

He's entered a space of pure, desperate need.

Without a sound I put my palm on his cheek. Permission and plea.

Take what you need. I want to fulfill you.

With a groan, he pushes into me, not particularly gentle. It feels too good. He's using me, fucking me, escaping into me. I find it unbearably hot. I must make some sound against his chest because he pulls back, kissing me again.

"More," he demands, rolling over and pulling me on top of him.

He's still feral this way. Still in control even though I'm on top.

I truly have no choice but to take what he gives me, to let him do what he wants, to surrender to his thrusts. I don't have to think about it. I don't have to worry. I don't have to manage. His hands and body and mind do the work. I'm something to be used. I'm begging by the time he grunts beneath me.

Climax rains over me like meteors, bright and fiery, destroying everything in its path. Every thought, every worry. I'm pure limitless pleasure as he fucks into me once, twice, three more times, his body hard against mine, locked tight for the final throes of orgasm.

Then I collapse on top of him. Beside him.

I'm breathing hard. My mind wants to drift off to sleep, but I can't do that. There's a man in my bed. Does he leave now? Do I invite him to sleep over? I have no idea. Sophia really needs to write a guidebook for women like me.

His large hand covers my breast. He strokes my nipple idly, casually. As if we have all the time in the world. Except we just had sex. I look at him, and he's gazing back, his expression almost predatory. "Are we doing this again?"

"I had to get it out of my system," he says. And it's not the cruel joke that someone can make it into when they pretend that fucking you once is enough. "Hard and fast and a little rough. Now I can do this." He kisses down the front of my body, and I am lost. How could I ever have survived anyone else but Finn Hughes? He makes me feel alive. I'm so full of pleasure that it's hard to contain in my body. He kisses down between my legs and when he buries himself there, I find myself gripping the covers, pressing my lips shut.

But then for what? It's my loft. I'm at home. There's nothing to hide here.

And in fact, there's nothing I *can* hide.

He's too close. He can see everything. He can taste everything, and he does. I'm out of practice, but that's because I haven't had sex with anyone since Lane. He loomed so large in my memory. Even after he broke my heart I assumed no one would ever compare.

I couldn't imagine someone like Finn.

Athletic. Adventurous. He seems like he could do this forever. He seems like he could go on and on all night—and what can I say? This is what I wanted. I never admitted it out loud, even to myself. But this is what my secret heart always wanted.

Someone who would not be unable to tear themselves away.

Someone who would choose me over everything.

Chapter Sixteen

Finn

I WAKE UP comfortable, which is a problem.

I normally wake up with a thousand things on my mind already. My to-do list haunts my dreams. My dad, my brother, the company. The list of my responsibilities. The list of my failures. But this morning as I come awake, I'm comfortable. A lazy kind of comfort.

My eyes stay closed, because I want to preserve the feeling.

Maybe it's a dream.

Then I feel her. The warmth across my chest. The faint silky strands of hair tickling my nose. An intense case of morning wood. Last night comes back to me with a rush of wild emotion. I enjoy sex as much as any man, but that was something different. It was uncontrollable, as if lust made my muscles move.

It drove me instead of logic, which is terrifying.

Part of me wants to gently move her aside, to slip out before she even wakes up. That would be the cowardly route. The other part of me wants to order a full brunch on DoorDash and spend the day in bed with her. The warring impulses make my heart pound.

I couldn't keep myself away from her last night. I fucked her several different ways, several different times, until finally she could take no more. She lay there, limp and sated, while I came for the last time. Then I collapsed next to her, where I stayed until morning.

Sunlight peeks around the edges of a thick curtain.

I'm fucked. I knew I shouldn't have come up here last night. I knew the right answer was to say no, to go back home and manage my house, and my life, and my family the way I always do. I knew and I did it anyway. Who the fuck am I becoming? I'm good at making these kinds of decisions. I'm good at knowing when I've reached my limit. I know how long I can be away from home. I calculate it down to the second. I know how long I can lose myself in drinks or games or people. I'm always back on time.

I'm past my limit with Eva.

Far past it, in fact. I have to admit that it feels good.

I anticipated that once I fucked her, the insane lust I feel around her would cool. Judging by the steel bar that is my cock right now, that isn't going to happen. She's soft and warm in her sleep. I want to slip inside her before she's even awake, to feel her slick and swollen around my cock, to rub her clit with my fingers so the first thing she knows on awakening is orgasm.

There's another impulse inside me. One that says she's at peace, and I don't want to do anything to disturb her. I've never been a man to deny myself pleasure. She would enjoy it, too. So why can't I make myself wake her up? Even as I burn for a touch of her velvety skin.

Christ. I'm well and truly fucked.

Eventually she stirs. Her body shifts in subtle ways until she becomes completely still.

She's remembering last night.

"Good morning," I say, my voice still scratchy with sleep.

She gives me a cautious, doe-eyed glance. "Good morning."

Now that she's awake, I give in to the urge to

touch her. To caress her. I run my hand up and down her arm. "I didn't mean to spend the night."

Embarrassment crosses her expression. "I'm sorry. I don't know the morning after etiquette. Am I supposed to make you coffee? Or look the other way while you get dressed?"

Fuck, she's so sweet. And strangely innocent. The world knows Eva Morelli as an incredibly smart and competent woman. This is a secret side of her. One only I get to see... for right now, anyway. Nothing lasts forever. Definitely not me. "You don't have to do a damn thing. But I can get out of your hair if you want."

"I'd like it if you stayed," she says, sounding almost shy. "This is nice."

"Then I'll stay."

She snuggles closer to me, curving her body against mine. The feel of her breasts makes my cock throb. I want to push her back and spread her legs and—

No. I force myself to wait, to revel in this different sort of intimacy. Rare in my world. And if I had to guess, rare in hers as well. It makes me curious about her sexual history. It's taboo to ask, but the speculation doesn't stop. She seemed hesitant last night. Not only because we were taking this to a new level, but also as if she wasn't used to sex. Maybe she hasn't had it all that often.

Maybe it's been a while. She could have even been a virgin, she was that tight.

"Did I hurt you?" I ask, my voice low.

Tension runs through her body. I stroke down her side, onto her lower back.

Maybe I was too rough with her. She could be sore.

Lord knows I had no control. No restraint.

"You didn't hurt me, but… it's been a while."

I force my voice to remain casual. "How long?"

"Fourteen years."

Holy shit. I'm propped on my elbow before I can stop myself, looking down at her. So much for sounding casual. "Are you fucking serious?"

"Yes." She blushes. "It doesn't matter. Why are you upset?"

"I'm not upset." I run a hand through my hair and tug. Hell. Maybe I am upset. "It's just that you should have told me. I would have been more gentle with you. I would have—"

"I didn't want you to be more gentle with me. I liked the way you were."

Her soft admission makes my cock throb. It reminds me that I have a very good view of her beautiful breasts, full and plush with dark tips. Desire yanks hard at my control. It would be so easy to have her right now. A distraction. It's a distraction from what I really want to know. "Why, Eva? You're beautiful, passionate, and very active in Bishop's Landing. How is it that no one can get you into their beds?"

She looks away, leaving me her profile. "Your father was right, okay? I did have my heart broken. No, he said it was shattered. And it's true."

I turn her chin back to me. "Who was it? And can I kill him?"

A pained laugh. "You can't. He's already dead."

Her words slam into me. I almost lose my breath. Is that why she's been single all this time? Been abstinent for fourteen years? Because she was in love and tragically lost him? It makes my chest feel tight to imagine her pining for him. Even as I licked her pretty sex, even as I fucked her so hard she saw stars, she loved a dead man.

"I'm sorry," I manage to say.

"It's not like that," she says, looking up at me. Her eyes have turned a paler brown in the morning light. Or maybe it's that she's baring her secrets right now that makes it seem that way. As if I'm looking past her defenses and into the heart of her. "I'm not still in love with him, but I was once. I wish I could shrug it off as childish infatuation, but if it had been that, I could have gotten over it. No. This was real, foolish, unthinkable, impossible, stupid love."

"What makes it stupid?" I ask softly.

I'm not against love. In fact, I want it. I want to experience it the same way as everyone else, with all the doubt, all the uncertainty. I don't want to know that I'll lose it by forgetting it ever happened. I don't want to saddle her with a childlike husband who screams at her when he gets confused at night. It's a sorry fate to face alone, but I won't take her down with me.

And considering how loyal she is to her family, if I *did* marry her for real, she'd probably stay with me to the bitter end. It's sad that my mother's left my father, but there's a kind of mercy in it, too. At least her memories of him are mostly from the past, when he was really himself. Eva would chain herself to her husband through sickness as in health.

"It was Lane Constantine."

Christ. Lane Constantine was married, though he was known for having affairs. And it would have been normal for him to have younger women as his mistresses, but still. Eva was so much younger than he was. "How old were you?" I say, struggling to contain my anger. If Lane weren't already dead, I would definitely punch him for taking advantage of her.

"Nineteen," she says, almost defensively.

Defending Lane fucking Constantine, as if that makes it okay. He would have been in his mid-forties by then. And she had been raised so sheltered, so Catholic.

That's not the worst part.

The worst part is that everyone knows he was mortal enemies with the Morellis. It's made for some creative guest lists and seating charts at Hughes events. We're connected to the Constantines via my mother, Geneva. Her sister Caroline married Lane.

We're also friends with the Morellis.

We don't pick sides in their little feud. With our power and fortune, we don't have to.

Then Lucian Morelli hooked up with Elaine Constantine.

Leo married Haley Constantine.

There's enough of a connection that the feud has cooled… for now. At one time, though, it was vicious. And Lane Constantine fucked his enemy's daughter. That's cold, even for ruthless billionaires. "Did he... hurt you?"

"No," she says quickly. "Nothing like that. At least not during...sex. He swept me off my feet, actually. I believed him when he said he loved me and wanted to leave his wife. I thought we could have some kind of fairy-tale ending."

My stomach knots. "That fucker."

Her laugh ends on an abrupt sob. "I thought we were like Romeo and Juliet, from two warring families, and we would find a way to be together."

"That story is a tragedy."

"Yes," she says with a soft sigh. "Yes, I figured that one out the hard way."

"Plus Romeo wasn't twenty five years older than Juliet."

She flinches. "Twenty-seven, actually."

I drop my head against her breastbone. She's so goddamn sexy. I swear my cock is going to get so hard it breaks right off. But I can't force myself to seduce her. This is a different kind of seduction, one where I lure information out of her. It's somehow more important than sex. "I'm afraid to ask but... how did it end?"

"We were together for nine months. We had fancy hotel suites and champagne. Sneaking around. I thought it was romantic." A caustic laugh. "I was stupid. He took me on trips outside the city. My parents thought I had a new internship. It seemed so real."

It seemed so real. Unlike what she has now.

I roll back onto my back and pull her against me.

She sighs with apparent relief. "And then I realized he was using me."

"How?"

"Like I said, I fell in terrible love. Enough that I told my best friend about it. My best friend, who was my brother. Leo told me that he'd had an affair with Caroline. And that Lane was only using me as revenge."

"Isn't he younger than you?"

She nods, averting her eyes. "I think Caroline was just using him to get back at Bryant. We became pawns in the fight between our parents."

Fuck. "I'm sorry."

"I confronted Lane."

"Did he admit it?"

A small shiver runs through her. Old pain. "Yes, but he said it changed along the way. Somehow he ended up falling for me for real. At least that's what he said. Maybe he was lying about that, too, but looking back, I think I believe it."

"You still stopped seeing him, though."

"Of course. I couldn't allow them to use me to get back at Leo."

Naturally she was more worried about her sibling than herself. "Of course."

"He kept calling, though. I think the connection was real between us, but it would always be tainted by how it started. He followed me to my college class one time. Leo found out and put a stop to it. I don't even know what he did, but Lane never talked to me again."

"Did you grieve when he died?" Every cell in my body rejects this idea.

"It was years later, but I guess… yes. I cried. It's not that I wanted to get back together with him. Or even that I still loved him. Love fades after a while. It was more like crying for me, for my brother, for the fact that neither of us could trust people. That was before he met Haley, though. She changed everything for him."

My heart clenches at the reminder of Haley with her false contractions and her husband's worry. "That will happen for you," I say, a knot in my throat. Of course I want her to be happy. To have a long, fulfilling relationship with a man who doesn't forget his own name. "You'll find someone, and it will change everything for you. You'll love again. And have a family."

She glances up at me, her eyes clouded with some emotion I can't name. "If you believe in second chances for me, why not you? You can have those things, too."

I don't bother trying to convince her. There's no time for that. No point, either.

We only have right now.

Her breasts finally capture my attention, and I nuzzle the gentle slope. Fuck, she's soft. I kiss a path around the outside curve and underneath, making her squirm, reveling in her panting breaths. When I close my mouth around her nipple, she moans her pleasure.

"Please," she whimpers.

Hunger rages inside me, an inferno through a field of gasoline. I've been holding back ever since I woke up. That's over now. I'll kiss her pretty pussy later. I'll make her come again and again, later. I'll spend time on foreplay later, because now I need to be inside her.

I spread her legs, but she puts a hand out to stop me. She stammers in an adorable way. "Shouldn't we be using a condom? I guess you're right. I don't have a lot of experience. I didn't even think of it earlier."

Every muscle in my body locks up. No. *No.*

"What the *fuck*?" I say. "How did we not use

one?"

Except I know the answer. I was crazed with lust. "I didn't think about it," she admits, looking guilty, as if it's somehow her fault that I fucked her raw.

I thought you could use protection this time. Because I didn't use it last night. That's never happened before. I always use a condom. Everyone knows to be safe these days, but I'm extra careful. It's not just about accidentally knocking someone up.

It's about creating a life that has my cursed genes.

If the disease only stripped years out of my life, that would be one thing. It does more than that. It will take my dignity. It's taken my father's dignity. He's a prisoner in his own mind. I swore a long time ago that I would never force that on someone.

Which means using a condom like it's a religion.

Last night Eva became my religion.

I push out of bed, away from her, away from the weakness she creates in me. My clothes are strewn around the room. I pick them up with jerky motions. Part of me recognizes that I'm acting abrupt. Surly, even. She doesn't deserve this behavior from me, but I feel too jittery inside to stop it. "I don't suppose you're on birth control," I say, not facing her.

"No." Her voice has cooled fifteen degrees. "I didn't need to be."

She wouldn't have needed it, not after being celibate for over a decade. I'm the one who's been having sex. I know enough to use protection. "Fuck."

"Listen," she says, and I look back to see her sitting up in bed. She has the white sheet pulled up over her breasts, as if she needs a shield. As if she needs protection from me. "I'm sure it's fine. It was only one time."

I give her a dark look.

"A few times," she amends.

I kept her up half the night, taking her again and again. "I'll send you a morning-after pill."

Her cheeks turn pink. "I'm sure I can find one on my own."

"And you can take a pregnancy test… I don't know when they start working." I know exactly fuck-all about pregnancy. "We'll figure this out."

She stands, and all the uncertainty is gone. The pain, the grief from her past? Gone. She's draped in a white sheet, looking like a goddess. Her shoulders are back, her chin held high. Her black hair spills around her bare shoulders.

Roman sculptors would beg to use her as their model.

"I'll be the one to figure this out," she says. "Which will probably be nothing at all. But either way, you're absolved. Released. So you can stop looking like someone shot you."

She crosses the room with the bearing of a queen.

"Eva." It occurs to me that I may have been intense in my reaction. People forget condoms sometimes. It's fine. Nothing happens. Like she said, it was only once. I probably could have asked her to take a morning-after pill without stomping around like an asshole.

Too late. The bathroom door closes in my face. I hear the sound of water being turned on. Steam begins pouring from the bottom of the bathroom door. She isn't coming back out anytime soon. And she sure as hell isn't inviting me to join her.

I'm pretty sure that was an invitation for me to fuck right off.

Chapter Seventeen

Finn,

I got your delivery, and I've taken it.

—Eva

Eva,

I'm sorry I lost my shit. Please forgive me.

—Finn

P.S. Let's go out tonight.

Finn,

Will you keep it wrapped up?

—Eva

Eva,

Yes, both my cock and my issues.

—Finn

Finn,

Come over.

—Eva

P.S. I'm holding this quarter from our bet hostage.

Chapter Eighteen

Eva

Leo's house looks like a castle, with rolling hills and a stone facade. There are even turrets. I arrive a few hours before the party armed with decorations and a large amount of cupcakes that are filled with colored frosting. So far only Leo, Haley, and myself know the gender of the baby. It will be a surprise to everyone else when they bite into the cupcakes that are topped with little books made out of fondant. *The Very Hungry Caterpillar. The Giving Tree. Goodnight Moon.* Books you read to children. Books Leo and Haley will read to their baby.

And in the middle there's pink frosting, to indicate a girl.

The house is already decked with balloon sculptures. The artist has been here for hours working on her installations, which feature pieces from the same books. A green and red caterpillar, a cow jumping over the moon.

I wave at her briefly before heading to the kitchen. Leo's regular chefs are handling the hors d'oeuvres, but I want to make sure they're doing okay.

And then I hear my mother's voice. Crap. She must have shown up early.

I take a hard left turn into the sitting area, where I find my mother facing off with Leo.

"We have to cancel," he's saying. "She's tired. She won't admit it, but I can tell."

"Everyone's already coming," my mother says, her voice shrill in a way that heralds a Category 5 hurricane. "My sister. Anita Barclay. Rosamund O'Connors."

"Then tell them not to come."

"It's too late for that," my mother says, half pleading. "We're going to look ridiculous if we cancel now."

Leo looks incensed. "So you're more concerned with appearances than the health of your first grandchild? Jesus fucking Christ, Mother."

"Leo," I say, my voice sharp enough for him to notice.

His dark glance communicates everything

about the situation—his frustration, his impatience. His fear for the wife and unborn child he loves. "What?"

"I need to speak with you. Privately. *Now*."

He reluctantly steps into another room with me. "I know you're the resident peacemaker, but don't tell me you're buying that bullshit. It's not your job to help our mother remain the social butterfly of Bishop's Landing, no matter how much guilt she lays on you."

The venom in his face takes me aback. "Leo. It's me."

He glares at me for another few seconds before dropping his head. "Jesus."

I approach him carefully and offer a small hug.

He squeezes me back, fierce and hard. "I'm sorry."

"It's okay."

It was easier to survive the gladiator arena that was the Morelli household if you had backup. So we formed little allegiances. Me and Leo. Lucian and Sophia. Carter and Daphne. Tiernan was the odd man out, because of the way our father raised him. And Lisbetta was still too young for most of it. Leo has seen me at my worst. He saw my devastation after things ended with Lane. And I witnessed him in his darkest hour.

"I'm afraid," Leo mutters, his voice low and hoarse.

"What's happening? Can you tell me?"

"Nothing. Everything. I don't fucking know. Haley says she's fine, but I see the way she looks at me. I don't think she'd really tell me if she were worried now. She thinks I'm being over the top, but what the hell else am I supposed to do?"

It's not a good thing if Haley feels like she needs to hide the situation from him. It means she could be very worried. It also means that Leo is being... overbearing. It's not that his concern is unfounded. It's that he approaches everything like his own personal crusade. If she's unwell, she needs support and love and care—not him starting World War III with our mother.

"Listen," I say. "I'll cancel the baby shower. I'll handle everything. You go upstairs and rest. Everyone will understand."

He paces away. "No. Haley said she wants the baby shower."

I wait, knowing he'll arrive there in his own sweet time. Rushing him won't help. "I promise no one will blame you if you cancel. I'll handle Mom."

A hard breath. "Fine. We're having it. But she

remains seated the entire time. Nothing that forces her on her feet. Nothing that might stress her out. And no opening presents. The last thing she needs is to get everyone's germs on her."

"Done," I say, my voice calm.

This is part of event planning. It's not all about food and drinks and decorations. It's about managing people under stress. Leo was always going to threaten to cancel the baby shower. And I was always going to wait it out. My mother should know that by now. Then again, she's never understood her children. It's something that frustrates her, and sometimes, in her private sorrow, pains her.

He gives me a hard look. "How's the engagement going?"

We talked on the phone after the infamous Morelli family dinner that he missed. That was two weeks ago. Two weeks of my family hounding me to set a wedding date. Or a huge engagement party, at the very least. Leo knows that it's fake, but he's worried about it.

That makes two of us.

When does this end? That question haunts me, along with the realization that I don't want it to end. Since that first night, Finn has spent almost every night at my loft, in my bed. First he takes me somewhere interesting in the city. Then we go back to my place. He's shown me new heights to sexual pleasure, things I didn't even think were possible.

And every night since then he's worn a condom.

He did end up sending a morning-after pill to my place, which I took.

It's almost a religion to him. And I understand why. We aren't really engaged. We aren't really together. It's fake, and I need to remember that. No matter how good it feels. No matter how intimate it feels in the moments we hold each other after sex.

He's always gone in the morning.

I wave my hand. "Don't think about that right now. We're going to have a nice, relaxed afternoon with friends and talk about fun baby stuff."

"Since when are the O'Connors friends? Mother hates them."

"She envies them, brother mine."

He shakes his head. "I know I'm being overbearing, but if anything happens to Haley…"

I don't give him platitudes. *Nothing will happen. Women have babies every day. It's totally natural.* Because I can't guarantee it will be fine.

Complications happen every day, too. When you've seen the darker side of life, you understand that. Even an upbringing sparkling with diamonds didn't shield us from that.

The next hour goes by in a whirlwind of preparation.

Then the guests start arriving.

Lisbetta, Sophia, and Bianca arrive together, bearing oversized pastel gift bags. I'm going to guess they hit the Disney store. Emerson brings Daphne himself, promising to pick her up when she texts. My mother greets her friends when they arrive. They drink mimosas and reminisce about their own children.

Elaine also shows up with a slim envelope, which I suspect holds something outrageous. Like buying a star for the child so that when space exploration becomes common, she'll already have real estate. She brings her sister, Vivian Constantine.

I'm not *quite* used to having Constantines around, but it's only fair.

This is Haley's baby shower. She should have people from her family.

However, I can't shake the hollow feeling when I greet Vivian.

I've gotten used to Elaine. I see her as a three-dimensional person. And my brother's wife. But I don't know much about Vivian, besides the fact that she's with the State Department. Something to do with the consulates, though I don't know what.

And, of course, she's Lane's daughter.

It doesn't escape my notice that we're the same age. I knew it before, on an abstract level, but we never spent time with the Constantines back then. It had seemed far away and irrelevant to our love.

She's completely nice when we talk, which shouldn't be a surprise.

I'm the one with the problem. She doesn't know why my heart is pounding and my palms feel sweaty. That's my own tell-tale heart pounding under the floorboards. I wasn't the only person Lane had an affair with, but that doesn't stop me from feeling shame. I was too young and naive to understand the ripple effects. And I was too gullible to believe him when he said it was something special between us.

Haley's sister Petra arrives with a toddler in tow, apologizing for an issue with the nanny. "It's no problem at all," I say, smiling at a bashful little boy with blond curls. "There's no shortage of laps for him to sit on."

Harlow is there, along with a few of Haley's friends from college.

Soon the baby shower is in full swing, with a tapas station, mocktails so the expectant mother can indulge, and a few games. As promised, Haley holds court from the formal living room, always seated, with Daphne at her side in case she needs something.

Leo glowers from the corner, clearly unconcerned with our 'no men' edict.

"Ambrose is here," he says when I try to nudge him from the room. Haley's nephew was finally coaxed from his mother's arms. He wandered off after Sophia some time ago. Knowing my sister, she's probably teaching him how to swear.

"Ambrose also isn't potty trained yet."

But I let my brother stay. Better that he keeps an eye on her.

She looks fine but tired. That's normal, isn't it? I hope so. I make sure Daphne keeps a glass of ice water nearby. Haley doesn't touch it, but I want her to stay hydrated. I'm not a doctor, but that just seems like a good idea.

Then it's time for the gender reveal.

Everyone is passed a cupcake on delicate china.

"Three," I say, holding up my cupcake. "Two. One."

Muffled exclamations follow as the guests see the pink filling, their mouths full of cupcake. Haley smiles in that serene way she's found while pregnant. She's always been a wise, steady presence, but pregnancy has taken her zen state to a new level. She accepts the congratulations and the endless advice in good humor.

Afterward, I shoo my sister Daphne away and take her place beside Haley. "Okay," I say, my voice private. "Tell me the truth. Are you tired? Exhausted? You can go upstairs now. Leo would be only too happy to carry you up there himself."

"No," she says, a hint of panic in her voice. "I can't survive another minute in that bedroom. There's no breathing room. I can't even blink without Leo offering me eyedrops or a cold compress or a heated blanket."

"Leo thinks you're understating it, though."

Guilt crosses her expression. "Maybe I am, a little. But we're already doing what the doctors told us to do. Having him worry more isn't going to help."

The cupcake I ate sits heavy and wrong. Probably because I was too busy to eat anything else. An empty stomach and sugar don't mix. "I don't want to intrude on your privacy, but what if I were to move in? That way I could distract Leo and give you some rest."

A faint smile. "The last thing you need is to spend more time managing Leo. Or any of the Morellis. You deserve some time for yourself. And," she adds with a sparkle in her blue eyes, "you must have found enough to fall in love with Finn Hughes."

My stomach flip flops. It *really* didn't like that cupcake. "Leo told you?"

Her voice drops to a whisper. "That it's fake? Yeah."

It's a big secret, but I didn't really expect Leo to keep it from his wife. They share everything. And it's a relief now to not have to hide from someone else. "I'm driving my sisters insane because I don't want to talk about it, but I don't know what to say. There's not going to be wedding colors and flowers and cake, and I can't lie to them about it."

"The whole relationship is a lie," she says, gentle but firm.

"It seemed harmless," I confess. "Something to make my mom stop looking for ready-made families for me—comes pre-built with a husband and children and three charity board positions."

Sympathy crosses Haley's face. "You should tell her to go to hell."

Hearing those words come from her mouth, when she's usually so sweet, makes me laugh. "Both our families have matriarchs," I say, referring to the dragon of a woman that is Caroline Constantine. "And you cross them at your own peril."

"Eva, Sarah isn't the matriarch of this family any more than Bryant is CEO of Morelli Holdings. You manage your parents' house. You're the one the kids go to when they need advice. I mean, you're even next in line to run Leo's company."

"I've *told* him we're not doing that. Not once he married you."

"It's okay," she assures me. "I'm going to have my hands full with the baby for a long time. And the truth is, I'm just not that interested in real estate. Either way I'll be taken care of. That's not the point, though. The point is that *you* are the matriarch of the family. You're the cornerstone. We all depend on you."

My heart thumps at the compliment. "That's sweet."

"It's true," she says, handing me her glass of ice water. She blinks a little bit, as if she's looking into the sun, though it's not too bright in here. "I do have a favor to ask."

"Anything." My stomach threatens to eject the cupcake. Come to think of it, I've been nauseous lately. I used to have protein shakes in the morning, but now I can barely stand the sight of them. What is going on with me?

"Don't let Leo drive," she says. "He's not going to be thinking straight."

"Don't let Leo drive where?"

That's when Haley closes her eyes and faints.

CHAPTER NINETEEN

Finn

I'M NOT USUALLY the type to rattle around my house. There's always something that needs to be done at Hughes Industries. Or someone in the family who needs or wants me to step in, like the situation with my aunt and the panda.

Somehow I find myself thumbing through volumes in the library, pushing them back when they're not what I'm looking for. What am I looking for? All I find is poetry.

Because I could not stop for Death –
He kindly stopped for me –

My grandfather was determined to avoid his fate. It didn't help.

My father was more philosophical about it. He collected poems and books and art about death, as if it was a test he studied for. The textbooks of that course fill these shelves.

As for me, I never thought to avoid it. Or accept it with open arms.

Instead I found solace in knowing that I would be alone at the end. No one else would watch me disintegrate. No one else would mourn.

Hemingway saunters into the room, still a little gangly as he grows into his height. He was an oops baby. My father had good days and bad days. My mother still lived in this house at the time, though he already had nurses and staff. She would absent herself when he turned manic and fretful.

My little brother was conceived on a good day, presumably.

My mom tried to stay after that, for the baby. She made it a few years.

Dad got worse and worse. Throwing things. Shouting. Sometimes he forgot who she was. Once he thought she was his nurse. Those were the hardest times.

Eventually she left to save her own sanity.

Hemingway throws himself into the heavy leather armchair across from mine, making it rock. That's what he does now. He throws himself into furniture instead of sitting. If my mother were around she would probably correct him. My father would say something about how a gentleman behaves. They aren't here, though. It's only me, and I remain quiet.

"Emily Dickinson," he says, reading from the volume I'm holding. "I had a language arts project about her. We had to analyze three poems, which were mostly about animals. Birds. Frogs. The occasional fly. Then we had to write a poem in her style about a topic that interests us. So I did one about my PlayStation."

"I didn't see that." I get regular reports from his teachers about his academic progress, as well as samples of his work. Not everything, though. I'd have to call the dean and change that.

He lifts his hand to the distant horizon like a Shakespearean poet and speaks.

I saw a world, in my head
And on the TV screen
It sang a song of violence—
Blood no one had to clean

"You wrote that? It's actually good. And insightful."

"Always with the note of surprise," he says with an exaggerated sigh.

"I'm mostly surprised you have a PlayStation. Didn't you lose your electronics privileges after the last time you were expelled?"

"I didn't come here to be interrogated," he says. "I came here to interrogate *you*. What's this about you and Eva Morelli? You're engaged?"

Christ. "I'm sorry. I should have told you about it."

"Ya think? I'm not even sure the engagement is legal if I haven't met her. Isn't she supposed to ask for your father's hand in marriage? Since Dad can't do it, I'll stand in. I have lots of questions to ask her."

"Very funny. And engagements *aren't* legal."

"Engagements are the path to legality, my friend. Marriage is forever."

Marriage is not forever. It's until I turn into a pumpkin. Then there's just an intelligent, generous, loving woman trapped with me. "My relationship with Eva is…complicated."

"That's what you call fuck buddies, Finn. Not your fiancée."

I groan at the reminder that I need to have an apparently very late talk about the birds and the bees with him. Since when does he use the term *fuck buddies*? He's growing up too fast at that boarding school. He didn't want to go, but Mom thought it would be best. She said that growing up around my dad would be too depressing.

She doesn't think I should live with him either.

The nurses handle his main care. The bathing and feeding. The daily walks for exercise. Sometimes they read to him or help with puzzles. Maybe it doesn't matter that I'm here most evenings. Or that I come home early and soothe him when he's in distress. But I can't help but think that if there's a chance that he's in there, if there's a part of him that's glad I'm here, then it's worth it. It doesn't escape my notice that I'm denying myself the same comfort I give him. There's some irony in that, I suppose.

"You know my feelings about marriage," I say.

Hemingway nods.

"And my feelings on children."

"Mhmmm," he says, drawing out the sound. Waiting for an explanation.

"My ideas about those things haven't changed."

"This is going to be a real surprise to the woman you proposed to."

It's impossible to explain what came over me at the Morelli family dinner. She was standing in the intersection of their lives, keeping them each from imploding. And I couldn't take it. I needed them to leave her the fuck alone. Or better yet, focus on what they could do for her. So I'd made up the lie. It was impulsive. Stupid. And strangely addictive.

Some perverse impulse inside me likes the lie.

"It's fake," I admit, blowing out a breath. "A fake relationship. A fake engagement. A way to get her family off her back. We enjoy each other's company. We respect each other. But we aren't really dating. And the truth is we aren't really engaged."

"Wow."

"I'd appreciate it if you didn't tell anyone."

"Who would I tell? My friends are back at Pembroke Prep."

There's bitterness in his voice.

Perhaps I've been expecting Hemingway to fend for himself during this absence. I check in on him a few times a day, and I've been working from home more to be accessible, but that's not the same thing as parenting. That's not the same thing as guidance. All the more reason not to become a father. I'm already a shitty older brother.

I've been distracted by Eva Morelli.

I set the book of poetry aside. "I can make a call to the dean. He's digging in his heels because he's a…" A homophobic asshole, to be specific.

It's not the sex in the bathroom that bothers him as much as that it was between two boys. "I'll make him see reason."

Money or threats. Those are the two things that make the world go round.

"Or," I say, keeping my tone casual. "Maybe you could move back home."

His eyebrows lift. "Really?"

"Only if you want to. I know it's probably more fun hanging out with boys your own age rather than me and dad. Our idea of a good time is meatloaf night."

He frowns. Looks away. Hesitates.

His nervousness shimmers in the air.

"Hem?"

"I really want to live at home." The words spill out in a rush, as if they've been pent up too long. "Everyone else does. They just drive in every day. It's only like forty-five minutes."

"I hadn't realized it bothered you."

He looks at me like I'm insane. "The only other kids who have to board are like foreign royalty, where their parents want them educated in the States but they have to stay in their home country. Or because their families hate them. That's what people assume about me."

Fuck. "That's not why you're boarding there."

An eye roll. "Because I'll be depressed if I live with my dad. Then why can't I live with her and travel the country, if she's that concerned about me? The actor in the new Batman movie, his kid goes to Pembroke, and she gets remote work when they travel."

It's a good point. "Okay. You can come back and live here if you want. I'll handle Mom."

Now I sound like Eva, handling the family. It's true, though. Someone has to. Maybe that's why I understand her so well. I know how responsibility drives you. Which sounds like a good thing, until you forget to eat or sleep or live your own life.

He grins. "Great."

It does feel surprisingly great, knowing he'll live here now. "Great."

"Now tell me the truth… you and this Morelli chick. Are you using protection?" He uses a low, imperious tone that I assume is what I sounded like when I asked him the same question.

Which is painful, because of course I didn't use protection the first time. Stupid of me. Impossibly stupid. I've used a condom every time after that, but I can hardly judge him for losing his head, since I did, too. "First of all, her name is Eva Morelli. You may call her Eva or Ms. Morelli, but not *that Morelli chick*. Secondly, none of your business."

"Then why is it *your* business if I use protection?"

"Where did you hear about it, anyway?"

"Someone sent me a post on Instagram. Apparently you're this influencer's soulmate and she wants to, and I quote, *cut a bitch* for making you fall in love. She was mostly joking, but she had enough violence in her eyes that I wouldn't trust Ms. Eva Morelli alone with her."

It's not ideal that social media has picked this up. We asked the family to keep it quiet, but it was only a matter of time before it got out. "If anyone asks you anything—"

"Don't comment. I've been a Hughes my whole life, you know. I know the drill."

"Right." I run a hand over my face. "Listen, I don't have a date tonight."

"Is she getting tired of you already?" he asks with exaggerated sympathy.

Actually, she had a baby shower this afternoon. No men allowed. It will probably run late, and she'll be tired after. Which makes me feel strangely itchy. I've gotten used to spending time with Eva. And spending part of the night in her bed. "Why don't we have a movie night?"

"You and me?"

"Sure," I say. "We could see if Dad's up to it."

"I want popcorn."

"I'm sure the chef can work something up."

A lopsided smile. "So, like a regular family movie night?"

"As regular as the Hughes ever get."

We head down the hall into the east wing, which is where my father lives. He has a set of apartments with connecting rooms for his nurses. Everything is soft and spare here. It used to be decorated like the rest of the house. One by one things have been removed. Vases when he knocked them over. Paintings when he tore one apart. A ten-thousand-dollar Rembrandt.

His nurse smiles when we enter, but it's not the good kind of smile. It's the smile that says she's already feeling sympathy for what we'll face with him.

I nod a greeting. "How's he doing?"

"Reactive, unfortunately. He's been a little emotional."

Which means outbursts, probably. Yelling. Throwing things. A movie night may not be in the cards. I step through the open threshold to a sitting area that contains a large TV. He's sitting in the middle of a couch, leaning forward, watching the screen while tear tracks glisten on his cheeks. What the hell? I come around to see what he's watching.

Fuck. It's a video from my birthday party.

I don't even know how old I was. Seven? Eight?

Dad set up an elaborate slip-and-slide system throughout the yard. Mom didn't stop moaning about the divots in the lawn for weeks, but it was worth it. In the video, children run through sprinklers and send their little bodies hurtling over plastic. I remember the crinkly feel of it, slick from the many hoses. I remember the scent of wet grass and the mud caked on my knees when I slid past the end. I remember laughing until my sides hurt.

Dad took lots of videos when we were younger.

They were like the poetry. Preparations for when he changed.

Memories for when he forgot.

The camera turns shaky, and then it's pointing at me. I'm grinning with a missing tooth. "Your turn," I tell the camera. "Dad, come on. You promised you would."

There's a faceless laugh. "Give me a minute, son. I have to do one thing before I absolutely destroy the grounds. I'm going to be in the doghouse for a long time."

My mother comes into view, looking torn between anger and laughter. "I'm not letting you in the house if you go down that slip and slide. You'll have to sleep in the gatehouse with the hounds."

The view shifts wildly, flashing briefly on a tableau of tables covered in food and balloon arches with people milling around. Then it jerks again, this time pointing at grass. "Are you sure?" Dad murmurs in a playful tone. "If I'm in the gatehouse, I can't make it up to you."

There's feminine laughter.

The screen goes black.

I turn around in time to see the remote sailing in my direction. I catch it before it hits me in the face. "Dad," I say, my voice thick from the memories. From the happiness I witnessed. Would they have done it again if they knew how it turned out? It doesn't matter. We don't get choices like that. We don't get do-overs.

"Get out," he says, his expression dark. "Get the fuck out of here."

Shit. It's one of *those* evenings. Movie night slips away.

He storms me, and I block him so that he

can't touch Hemingway. He swings wildly and connects with the side of my jaw. Fuck. That might bruise. Which will be fun to explain to people. "Dad, calm down. Nothing is wrong. You're safe. It's me."

"You." Foaming spittle forms at the sides of his mouth. "*You*. As if I'm supposed to know who you are. Well, I don't. You're a stranger. Who the hell are you, and where is my family?"

"I'm your family," I say, my voice gentle.

It doesn't help. He fights harder, though I'm not even sure what he wants. To get past me? To hurt me? "Where's my wife? Geneva? *Geneva?* Where's my son? Where's Finn?"

"I'm Finn, Dad. I'm right here."

He glances back at the TV wildly. "No, that's Finn. That's my son."

I glance to where Hemingway stands, stricken. "Go on. I'll come in a little bit."

"Where is she?" my dad says, sounding broken. "Is she dead? Just tell me. Please. Are my wife and son dead? Am I in an insane asylum? Is this hell?"

Despair clangs like a church bell. *Is this hell?*

Maybe it is. No one would choose to live like this.

"She's not dead," I manage to say. "Neither is

dead. They're both safe and healthy. The reason why you can't see Geneva is because... because you're separated."

Shock. Hurt. Anger. "You're lying to me. You're a liar, and you're holding me prisoner. I won't stand for it. Geneva," he shouts. "Are you okay? Can you hear me?"

"Mr. Hughes," Hemingway says, pushing past me. "I'm here for an interview. Your secretary said you could see me now. I appreciate the opportunity."

My father looks bewildered for a moment.

He looks down, as if surprised to find his hands grabbing me. He releases me by small degrees, finally stepping back. "An interview? At my home? This is highly unusual."

Hem gives his signature smile. "I'm an unusual candidate."

"Yes," my father mutters. "Well, if my secretary sent you over, it must be important."

Together we move my father into a different room, the black screen a distant memory. "Thank you," I mutter to Hemingway. "And sorry about movie night."

"No problem. You know, I think it's easier for me. This person is the only Daniel Hughes I've ever known. That guy behind the video camera? I never even met him." He glances back at me. "You better put some ice on that while I talk about my five-year plan. If it makes you too ugly, Eva Morelli won't want to look at you."

Chapter Twenty

Eva

The Hughes estate can fit both the Morelli and Constantine estates.

That's in line with how much money and power they have as well. The drive doesn't even go up to the front door. Instead I enter a circular drive that opens up to a heavily landscaped courtyard. Gazebos and old-fashioned lampposts lead the way to a grand mansion. Two curved stone staircases on either side lead up to a space with marble floors encircled by Corinthian columns.

Above the ceiling is more railings, where people can look down from parties.

A chandelier hangs in the center, alight at all hours.

It was a spontaneous decision to come here. I

stand outside a set of massive double doors that are twice as tall as me. It takes a lot to intimidate a Morelli, but this has done it. It's like a palace. When Finn brought me here before, we came in the back way. A family entrance.

The front is designed to emphasize their position to visitors.

Why did I come here? This is Finn's home. This is where he takes care of his father. Where his brother is staying after getting expelled.

I'm an intruder.

If I had any doubts about whether Finn wants something longer lasting with me, a true relationship, they were dashed when I saw how he reacted to the missing condom. It was more than concern. It was a deep, agitated regret. He doesn't see a future with me.

Our engagement isn't real. I don't belong here.

I'm turning to leave when the door opens. A man stands there. I recognize his clothes and his bearing, even if we've never met before.

"Miss Morelli," he says in a solicitous voice that contains a faint English accent. "Won't you come in?"

He probably saw me on the Nest cam or something. No doubt there's security and cameras all over the grounds. Heavily encrypted, of course. Very secure.

Their secrets need to be protected.

"I came to see if Finn is at home. Or if he's busy."

"Please come in," he says, holding the door open. "I'll take you to him."

I remain on the expansive front patio, even though I'm being strange. "You know what? He might be busy. I didn't call ahead. Maybe you could check before I just—"

"Eva?" Finn comes down one of two large staircases, looking so handsome it stops my heart. His hair is ruffled. He wears a dark blue sweater and slacks that's casual for a man usually in suits. He looks tired, but that only adds to his realness.

This is a flesh-and-blood man. Not a dream.

"I'm sorry," I say, flustered. "It's just that I—"

He reaches me, concern in his expression. "Is everything okay?"

I look down and realize that I'm still wearing a ruffled lavender dress. I bought it specifically for Haley's baby shower. Which feels like a million years ago. I packed Leo into the ambulance, making the EMTs swear not to stab him no matter how intensely he acted. Then I piled into an SUV with my sisters to go to the hospital.

It took a few hours for them to run every test in existence.

I'm pretty sure Leo thought of a few more just to drive them insane.

She fainted, the doctors said. Relatively normal. At least that's what they tried to tell us. Haley is officially on bed-rest, which means she really is trapped in that bedroom. Though the doctors aren't particularly worried, she can't walk around if she might faint.

The fall could hurt her.

Leo didn't accept the explanation of *relatively normal*. He then insisted the head of Obstetrics for the entire hospital group fly to New York City. Emerson came to pick up Daphne. Lucian took Elaine away. Sophia and Lizzy were each driven home.

I remained until the end, escorting them back home, smoothing over Leo's sharp words with the hospital staff and driver. I kept him from losing it completely when we arrived at the house and his deepest fears overwhelmed him. Hospitals. Pain. Death. Haley was tucked into bed, Leo in a chair beside her, his eyes rimmed red, his expression grim as he stared at his wife, by the time I left.

Somehow I didn't drive back to my loft.

I ended up here.

The fear of that moment, of watching Haley sink into a faint, of not knowing how she or the baby would be, comes to me in a rush. I had to be strong for Leo, for my family. That's over now. The facade drops. There's room for my emotions with Finn. I can be vulnerable here. I can be safe here. It comes upon me all at once. I break into uncontrollable, messy sobs.

Strong arms surround me. I recognize them as Finn's.

I have the strange thought that I would always recognize them, because of how safe he makes me feel. Except *always* doesn't last forever. Which makes me cry harder.

He half-carries me across the stone and down a few steps. I'm aware of crossing an open space. A few more stairs, and then Finn sits.

I'm wrapped in his lap, being held, his lips pressing in an unending kiss against my temple. I let all of my fear come out in those cries—not only for my niece and Haley and Leo, but for my entire family. For everyone I care about, when it feels like they're always on the brink of breaking. Like if I look away, if I blink, they'll come undone.

I'm the one coming undone.

Slowly the sobs taper off, leaving only shudders.

We're still outside. I can smell the salt scent of the water. The Hughes estate backs up to Stony Cove beach, where the earth comes together. Mountain and ocean and land interlace their fingers. It gives us privacy. It feels like we're in our own world.

"Tell me what happened," he murmurs.

"Nothing," I say, my voice thick. "She's okay. Haley's okay. The baby is okay." The words are more than conversation. They're a prayer.

"Okay," he says, his voice still calm and soothing. "That's good."

I let out a deep breath. "She collapsed at the baby shower. Something about how the hormones released in the body during pregnancy relax the blood vessels. Low blood pressure means less oxygen to the brain. So she fainted."

He rubs my back in calming circles. "Did she get hurt?"

"I caught her. She was dead weight in my arms. I had her on the couch before Leo got to me." A soft laugh. "I think he broke the light and sound barrier doing it. Apparently the biggest thing to worry about is being hurt from the fall, so they put her on bed-rest."

"I'm sorry. Can I do anything to help?"

I lean my head against him, and he tucks me under his neck. "You always see me at my worst. Things going wrong. Breaking down. Crying."

"I see you at your best," he says softly. "Every time."

My heart squeezes. "I know she's okay. My brain knows it, but my heart can't seem to—"

"Of course not," he says, his voice low and calmly reasonable. "Adrenaline flooded your system, helping you handle it. For hours. And once it wears off you need rest."

I sigh. "I should probably call my mother and give her an update. I talked to her when Haley was discharged from the hospital, but I should still—"

"Can you send her a text?"

"Well, I suppose. But she already knows all the information. She'll just want to decompress. Talk it out until she feels better."

Silence from Finn.

Then: "You need to feel better, Eva."

I stiffen. "They're my family. This is a crisis."

"Earlier was a crisis. This is you serving as the emotional regulator for every person in your family. If your mother is stressed, that's fine. A scary thing happened. Let her be stressed."

"I should be there for her."

"Will she be there for you? Or does it always go one way?"

Indignance rises. "I know the Morelli family is messed up. I know we're broken and toxic and a million other things, but they're mine. I love them, and they love me."

"They love what you do for them."

That's it. I stand up, even though it hurts to leave the warm comfort of his arms. And I face him in my rumpled lavender baby shower dress. "You're one to talk. You're sacrificing your entire life to your family. And not just your family. That I could understand. You're sacrificing everything to the *secret* your family keeps."

"Eva."

"You're just as bad as me. Admit it."

"It's not the same."

"It's worse, actually."

"It's the Hughes curse. I was raised to do this."

"Phineas Galileo Hughes, your family doesn't have a lock on curses."

He pauses. "I like my name on your tongue."

I glare at him, because I'm still not over it. He gives everything to his family and then tries to argue when I want to do the same. Both of us tend our families like they're terrariums, ecosystems that only exist because we're keeping them together.

"It makes me hard," he says, tracing two fingers down my thigh, along the silk fabric of the dress. "But I never got to sign it on your naked body the way you did on mine."

Sensation runs through me, hot and electric. "I'm still mad at you."

His lips quirk. He's still the playful Finn I knew all this time, but there's more gravity in his eyes now. More awareness of the pull between us. "You'll forgive me, though."

"Are you so sure of yourself?"

"When are you going to see it?" He pulls me by the backs of my thighs until I'm standing in front of him. He's still sitting on the wooden seat of the gazebo, in those damned casual clothes, a navy sweater that conforms to broad shoulders and muscled arms. "I'm not sure of myself, sweetheart. I'm sure of you. You're too damned loyal for your own good."

He says it in a rueful way, as if it's a weakness.

I have something to say to that, an argument to make, but it flies out of my head as soon as his hand slips beneath my dress. Up and up to where a lavender garter belt holds up my hose. My breath catches when he brushes the inside of my leg.

Something dark on his jaw catches my attention. I reach out and stop short, not wanting to hurt him. "Did something happen? Did you get into a fight?"

A short laugh. "Something like that."

"Finn?"

"It was a rough night," he admits. "Dad only got to bed an hour ago. Hemingway helped. A lot. We both collapsed when it was over."

Dismay makes me frown. "And then I came here to dump my feelings on you."

Two fingers hook into the hem of my panties. "I want your feelings."

"You must be tired. You—"

"Not too tired for this," he says, tugging my panties down.

I step out of them without even thinking, as if we've been doing this forever, him undressing me in a moonlit gazebo, his hazel eyes dark. "Are you sure?"

He lifts my leg and puts my foot on his cock, which is hard and throbbing beneath his slacks. "Does this feel like I'm sure?"

My toes wriggle, and he grunts.

"Fuck," he mutters, then moves my foot to the bench beside him. He slips down to the slatted floor, so he's looking up at my dress from underneath, his face inches away from my sex. My breath catches. He's too close, too intimate. I feel shy. I try to pull away, but strong hands haul me back. They knead my ass, a little too rough. It's perfect.

Both of us ran an emotional gauntlet today.

Physical touch feels like a balm. The harder the better. Make me feel it. Make it hurt.

He kisses a line along the inside of my thigh, and I whimper. No. No. *Yes.*

I'm standing with one foot on the floor of the gazebo, the other on the bench. Completely exposed to his hands. His mouth. He presses a hard, open kiss to my pussy, and I sob. It's like crash landing on earth after fearing you'd never come home. It's pain and relief together. My hips rock in an ancient motion, riding his tongue.

He builds me up to the breaking point and then stops.

It's cruel.

"Please, Finn."

"You beg so pretty," he says, his voice low. "Do it again."

"Please make me come," I say, desperate, my voice echoing off the water.

His tongue circles my clit, and I come with

violent shudders and hoarse cries. I would fall to the ground if he didn't hold me up. He moves my body as if I weigh nothing. He turns me around so I'm facing the bench. Blindly I reach out and hold the railing. Wood grain imprints onto my skin. He lifts my hips until I'm standing. I hear behind me the tear of a condom wrapper. Even now he's safe. We won't lose our minds again. Even in the middle of a hurricane, we're protected. Then he plunges inside me, and I cry out.

"Yes. More. Please."

"That's right," he says in a growl. "Eva Morelli, who handles everything and everyone. Eva Morelli, the queen of goddamn Bishop's Landing. And here you are getting railed. You love it, don't you? My cock inside you? Your pussy's sucking me like a goddamn mouth."

I whimper. "Finn."

"You know who makes you feel this good. It's me, isn't it? It's always me."

Then he comes, his fingers tightening painfully on my hips, a roar behind me. The pulse of his cock inside me pushes me over the edge, and I cry out, free falling, even as I cling to the gazebo's railing, losing myself in the rapture that shouldn't be real.

Chapter Twenty-One

Finn

I'VE SLEPT WITH Eva in her bed plenty of times, though I don't linger. I usually head home when the first rays of summer sun peek over the skyscrapers so I can be home before Hemingway wakes up. I've never woken up with her here, though.

And somehow, it feels more real.

Visiting her loft is like being a tourist in a beautiful foreign country. I could enjoy my time and then return, leaving it behind. This is in the same house where I've lived my entire life.

The same house where I plan to die.

I pull her closer as if it can keep time from taking her away. She'll go either way. That much I'm sure about. I can keep this fake now, and she'll walk away. Or I can wait until the bitter end.

I can make her feed me and bathe me. I can make her a shell of her former self, and then, only to save what's left of herself, would she finally leave.

Actually, seeing how she is with her family, she wouldn't even leave then.

I'd take her down with me.

I would steal her future the same way the curse stole mine.

"Finally awake," she says, her breath stirring the hair on my chest.

"How long have you been up?"

"Not a long time, but I didn't want to move. This felt too good." She moves to get up, pulling away from me before I can stop her. "Though I can get out of here, if you want. Before Hemingway sees me."

"No, I—" I sit up, capturing her hand. "I told him about us. I told him it's not real."

Some emotion crosses her face, but it's gone before I can grab it.

"He found out about the engagement on Instagram somehow." Embarrassment flickers through me. I'm the one who made the lie, but I couldn't even follow through. "He's had an unsteady family life. I didn't want him to think

I'd really have gotten engaged without him having met you."

A flush touches her cheek. She's turned away from me, so I can only see the expanse of her back, the slender column of her arm, the dark tip of her breast. Her black hair spills around her like a veil, shielding her.

But I can see it anyway, despite her hair and her poise.

I'm hurting her.

Every time I say that our relationship is fake or that our engagement is pretend, it hurts her. She always looks away so I can't see it in her eyes, but I see it now. It's in the angle of her head, the heaviness of her heart. I was worried about hurting her in some distant future, but it's happening right now. It's already here.

"We're a hashtag," she says.

"A what?" I ask blankly, still stunned from my realization.

"It's a mashup of our names. #Finneva."

"Christ."

"There's also a TikTok sound."

"Listen, Eva. I know I'm the one who sprung this engagement on you. And the one who came up with the whole idea of fake dating in the first place. And I want you to know that—"

My phone rings with a tune that jolts me. There are only a few callers who can make that sound, and they're all my father's nurses and support staff. I hit *answer*, and a breathless voice says, "Mr. Hughes? I'm sorry to bother you, but—"

In the background I can hear yelling.

I'm out of the bed in seconds, reaching for my slacks from last night and a fresh white T-shirt. "Coming," I say before ending the call. "I'm sorry. I have to go. There's—"

Eva's already rummaged through my drawers. She comes up with a pair of boxer briefs and another white T-shirt like mine. "Let's go."

"Stay here."

"I'm coming with you. Don't worry about me."

Without arguing further, I turn and head down the hallway.

Whatever is happening right now, she shouldn't see it. Then again, doesn't she already know the worst of me? Then again, maybe she doesn't. Maybe she's romanticized it into something it's not. She doesn't know about the way fear and paranoia can take hold of him. They make him lash out. One nurse was punched in the face. He tore her cornea and fractured her nose.

That's when we moved to two nurses per shift, minimum, at all times. Part of their jobs is to protect the other person. They have strict orders to do whatever's necessary to defend themselves, even if it harms my father. I won't let him hurt another person.

She doesn't know about the time he smeared his shit into the wallpaper. Or the time he pulled out his own breathing tube before the nurse could sedate him. He may have the reasoning skills of a child, but he has the body of an adult. We can't restrain him. It's considered inhumane, but sometimes…

Sometimes even existing in his state is inhumane.

We reach the apartments to find both nurses struggling with him.

The irony is that he loses sensation in his extremities. Which means he literally feels less pain. That makes him impossibly strong, even as he injures himself.

I rush past them and take him into my arms. It's a delicate balance, keeping him from hurting himself while also keeping him from launching himself into the room. Or at one of the nurses. I have the briefest fear about Eva. She won't know to defend herself from him. But I manage to get him onto his bed.

I'm still holding his arms, waiting to see if he'll fight me. I look into his eyes, hoping he can see me past the fever-bright fear. "Dad. *Dad.* It's me. It's Finn."

His familiar brown eyes are cloudy. "Who?"

"It's Finn. Phineas. I'm your son. Remember?"

"I don't—" His eyebrows draw together. "Do I know you?"

I swallow hard around a knot in my throat. It's not the first time he's ever gotten confused, but it's hard to face after the raw emotion of my night with Eva. My defenses are down. "You taught me how to hit a baseball. And take apart a computer. And fly an RC plane, even though we lost three of them in the ocean."

He looks bewildered. And sad. "I'm sorry, young man. I don't know you."

Sorrow rises like a tidal wave. It pricks the backs of my eyes.

"That's okay," Eva says, coming forward. She looks adorably tousled in a large white T-shirt, only the bottoms of my briefs visible from beneath its hem. "I'll tell you about him."

"You will?"

She sits on the edge of the bed and takes his

hand in hers. It's not a gnarled hand. Not arthritic. No age spots. He isn't old enough for that. It's just a regular male hand made more frail because he doesn't like to eat. The doctors tweak his diet daily to try and pack more calories in. I worry for a moment that he'll lash out, but he seems calm enough. And curious.

"Phineas Galileo Hughes," she says as if she's telling a story that starts a long, long time ago. And I suppose it does. "Phineas is a name on the Hughes side, I believe. An uncle."

"He was a pirate," I offer, my voice husky.

She glances back, a half-smile on her face. "A pirate?"

"A privateer during the Revolution, technically. There are rumors of a map."

"You named him after a pirate and an astronomer," she tells my father, who looks bemused but seems to be settling into this conversation. Whatever sent him spiraling is long forgotten under the sweetness of Eva's presence. "Which means, I think, that you wanted him to have adventures. And to look up at the stars."

I find myself captured by the sight of her, earnest and true. She's done more than calm him. She's calmed me. I never really thought about my names, aside from the fact that there were heavy expectations. And the fact that I got into fights over my middle name in boarding school. I didn't realize my father could have wanted me to sail the seas.

"They go together," I say softly. "Sailing and the stars."

She glances back and smiles. "You do enjoy breaking the rules."

"Hey," I say, gently chiding. "I'm a very upstanding person."

"Okay, *Phineas*," she says, teasing. She turns back to my father. "He enjoys things that are dangerous. Fast cars and illegal betting and underground boxing matches."

"And dangerous women," I say, my voice low.

"And thoroughbred horses who win races."

"Though not precisely in that order."

"He does those things because he's running out of time. At least he thinks he is. And he's so determined to experience everything, like maybe he can leave it behind. Like if he's felt every emotion, every risk, every thrill, he'll accept it when it's time to go."

My throat closes. She has me figured out.

You're sacrificing your entire life to your family. And not just your family. That I could understand. You're sacrificing everything to the secret *your family keeps.*

Is it true? Maybe.

It's more than a wish, though. My father made me promise. It wasn't just when I was six, seven, eight years old. It was later, when he would still have lucid moments. He would find me in the middle of the night, wake me up, and make me swear not to tell anyone. Ever.

The poetry didn't help him then.

All the risks I take now won't help me later.

"Are you afraid?" The question comes from my father. At first I think he's asking Eva, but his questioning gaze is on me.

"Maybe," I say, answering honestly. I put my arm around Eva's shoulder. "Sometimes it does feel like I'm running out of time, and I don't know the right way to handle that. I don't know how to face it without letting the knowledge change me. How do you walk into battle without armor?"

"It can change you," my father says. "It can change you for the better."

I shake my head. Not a refusal. I don't even know what better would mean.

"Kinder," my father says, seeing the confusion on my face. I can tell from his expression that he still doesn't recognize me. I'm not his son right now. I'm a stranger to him, just like this version of him is a stranger to me. Though maybe it's not. I've gotten to know this person for years. Maybe some part of this version recognizes me. "It can make you kinder. More loving. More giving. What's the point of holding back if you're going to lose it all in the end?"

It sounds so reasonable when he says it, but he doesn't even know what we're talking about. I look deeper into his eyes, as if I can find my father looking back at me. Instead it's this other person, the only one that Hemingway ever met.

"He is kind," Eva says, still holding my father's hand. She looks at him, not me, as she speaks. "And loving. And giving. He's a good man, your son. A great one."

My father's cloudy brown eyes struggle to focus.

His eyelids droop.

The nurse steps forward with another blanket.

Eva stands back to allow her space. My father's hand slips out of hers. I take Eva and pull her into my side. "Thank you," I say, my voice thick.

"You're welcome." She hesitates like she wants to say more. Then she speaks in a rush. "Finn, it doesn't have to end this way. With you alone and scared in this room."

So we're really going to do this. "Of course I wouldn't be in this room. He'll be here. I'll be in my own rooms. See, most likely he'll still be alive when I lose my grip on reality. It's only our brains that give up in our thirties. Not our bodies. We live a long time this way."

"Good," she says fiercely. "Do you think I'd want you to pass away early just because you have an illness?"

"Why wouldn't you? I want it. Every man in my family has had to weigh that stone." Even my father had done that. Not all of the poems involved a nice carriage ride with Death. Some were about suffering and the way out. Suicide.

Eva's eyes go wide. "That's not funny, Finn."

"I'm not joking, Eva."

Her eyes fill with tears. "Please don't."

"I'm still here," I say, my tone caustic as I spread my arms wide. The ironic showman. "In all my glory. Stockholders everywhere are safe as long as I'm alive."

Her dark eyes shimmer. "I know I'm not supposed to care about you. None of this is real, but the truth is that I love you."

Brittle silence follows the declaration.

My father slumbers peacefully on the bed.

The nurse has stepped outside to give us privacy. We're standing in what will be my future prison. She was right when she said I see myself here.

"I'm twenty-nine," I say, my voice low. "My dad's first episode? He was thirty-six. That's in seven years."

"Then give me seven years," she whispers. "Or even less than that. Give me seven months. Let me earn your trust. I won't abandon you, Finn. No matter what."

It's a gut punch.

I won't abandon you, Finn.

Of course she won't. She's loyal down to her core.

No matter what.

Even if it breaks her.

She won't leave me…unless I make her.

"I'm sorry if you thought this could be more," I say, my voice low. "I tried to be clear that it was fake. That it could never be real between us."

She flinches, and I feel like a bastard.

Because I am a bastard.

I run a hand over my face. "It's not you. God, Eva. You're so strong. So beautiful. So generous. If it were anyone, it would be you. But I can't—"

"You can if you want to."

Of course Eva Honorata Morelli would call

me out on my bullshit.

"You're a grown man," she says. "An impossibly competent, strong, powerful man who's choosing to live alone so you don't have to be afraid, but it doesn't work like that. You've already put yourself in that room with him. You've already isolated yourself."

"That's my choice," I say, my voice hoarse.

It's a choice I made years ago.

Before her.

And it will remain my choice long after she's gone.

She hesitates like she wants to argue with me. Eva doesn't give up easily. She's not used to failing when she puts her mind to something.

Which will only get worse the longer this goes on.

I have to end it.

"You already fell for me." My tone is cold. "And that's the danger. You can't get back all the love you spend on other people. It's impossible. You've made another mistake, Eva. I'll forgive you for it. The question is whether you'll forgive yourself."

She takes in a little breath. She's not the one who needs forgiveness. It's me. I never should have agreed to this. I never should have let things get this far. And they have gone so far. She's seen my father. She's seen our house. She's slept in my bed. I can feel walls going up around my heart in a futile attempt to protect me. It won't.

This will all come back to haunt me. It's already haunting me. I am a haunted man while I'm still alive. A cursed man. That's what it is to live under a curse. You never know when it might strike. So you might as well let it come down on you. Take it before it can take you.

"I don't want it back," Eva says, but her voice trembles. She hasn't moved away. And I wonder if that's because she can't or because she's frozen here with hurt. If she wishes more than anything that she'd never come here, that she'd never come with me after the gala for the Society for the Preservation of Orchids, that she'd never met me at all.

"You think you love me? No. You don't even *like* me. You don't like charming men, remember? And that's the one thing I am: charming."

Her eyes are impossibly black. Darker than night. They should be opaque, but somehow I can see the pain inside. I can see the old heartbreak I brought up to hurt her. Lane Constantine was the charming man she learned not to trust. I brought it up to push her away, but I have to make sure she never comes back.

I look Eva Morelli directly in her beautiful, dark, sad eyes, the ones I've thought about for months. The ones I want to think about forever. "It's over, sweetheart. We had a good time, but that's all this ever was. I wish I could say I'll miss you, but the truth is that I won't. In a few short years, I won't even remember you existed."

Chapter Twenty-Two

Eva

This is the worst I've ever felt.

Heartbroken. Worn out. Slightly hungover, even though we didn't drink last night. Maybe it's just an emotional hangover, but it feels as real as anything.

Damn it. It was good to be in his bed.

Better to be in his arms.

And the best thing in the world to be there for him when he needed me.

Now all I can hear is his voice. *It's over, sweetheart. We had a good time, but that's all this ever was. I wish I could say I'll miss you, but the truth is that I won't. In a few short years, I won't even remember you existed.*

I feel worse than I did fourteen years ago. In my youth I believed I was in love, but it wasn't real. It was infatuation and perhaps even a little bit of daddy issues. Now I'm older. I can tell the difference between what's fake and what's love.

What I feel for Finn Hughes is love.

That doesn't go away no matter how badly he hurt me.

The farther my driver gets from the Hughes estate, the worse I feel. I'm not prone to getting carsick. Now every turn makes me queasy. My stomach threatens to revolt, though I didn't eat breakfast. What the hell?

I crack one of the windows and breathe cool, fresh air.

My stomach calms a little, but I'm still heavy with other emotions.

My lavender clutch contains my cell phone and my credit cards. But it's now short by twenty-five cents. I left the quarter on his bedside table. The original quarter that he tossed to me in a bet.

I suppose I could add foam to my Starbucks order tomorrow.

There won't be any foam for me. It wasn't a good time, after all.

It's heartbreak, but something else.

Dread.

Some detail I'm missing.

Which is out of character. I don't miss details.

Things don't just slip my mind. I suppose in all the chaos around the fake engagement and the baby shower, something *could* have. An appointment? A meeting I've scheduled in the next fifteen minutes?

I fumble for my phone.

The sensation sets in. I'm late for something. But there's nothing on the calendar for today.

It would be normal to curl up and sob about what Finn did.

Heartbreak hurts, but this is...

More.

It feels like my loft is getting caught in a tornado. All my great-aunt's antiques smashing to the floor. It feels huge and uncontrollable. Not like my emotions normally are. Except when it's that time of the month.

Except...

When it's that time of the month.

My hand freezes on the phone.

A notification from my period tracker app pops up.

Has your period started yet? Don't forget to log it. :)

Ha.

No. That's not happening. It can't be happening, because Finn Hughes is the only person I've had sex with in over a decade, and Finn Hughes isn't going to have children. We slipped up one time with the condom, but I took the morning-after pill. We used each other for what we needed, and now he's done with me. It doesn't matter how real it got.

You can't get back all the love you spend on other people. It's impossible. You've made another mistake, Eva. I'll forgive you for it. The question is whether you'll forgive yourself.

Okay.

Now I'm going to throw up.

I'm barely holding it together by the time I'm dropped off at my building.

Outdoor air restores me, at least a little. I'm no longer in imminent danger of being sick on the sidewalk.

I go through the lobby of the building like a ghost, nodding at the doorman and accepting a nod from security. The dread doesn't lift in the elevator. Or even when I step into my loft. My private place since I was nine. My haven.

When the door is closed behind me, my eyes land on the settee. What is it I said to Lizzy? *We'll take a test, and then we'll know for sure.*

Right.

That's all there is to it.

Take a test. Know for sure.

I can't do anything until I have more information. It will probably be negative, anyway. And then I'll just go from there. Like I always do.

Luckily, the tests come two to a box, so I don't have to make another call down.

It's waiting there, vaguely accusatory, in my bathroom cupboard. Peeing on a stick is really not the way I thought I'd process Finn breaking up with me. I've done less dignified things in my life, but those were for other people, not for me.

The instructions say to wait for three minutes.

Lizzy couldn't look at the test, but I can't look away. There's nobody to knock on the door and read the results for me.

It's not you. God, Eva. You're so strong. So beautiful. So generous. If it were anyone, it would be you. But I can't—

It doesn't take three minutes.

The second line appears right away.

When the timer on my phone rings, it's a dark, inescapable pink.

I'm pregnant with Finn's baby.

Fuck.

✧ ✧ ✧

Thank you for reading ONE FOR THE MONEY! We hope you loved the steamy, emotional rollercoaster of Finn and Eva. What will Finn do when he learns that she's pregnant? Find out what happens next in TWO FOR THE SHOW.

Pregnant. Alone. And heartbroken. The only thing Eva Morelli knows for sure is that she wants this baby. She learned how to depend only on herself a long time ago.

The father, however? He made his position on marriage and children very clear.

Finn Hughes has fought his fate for years, but it's finally catching up to him. Duty took away his choices. How can he hope for forever? He already knows how this ends.

There's only one thing worse than having a family.

Losing them.

Other books about the Morelli family include:
- Lucian and Elaine in HEARTLESS
- Tiernan and Bianca in DANGEROUS TEMPTATION
- Sophia and Damon in CLAIM

The warring Morelli and Constantine families have enough bad blood to fill an ocean, and their brand new stories will be told by your favorite dangerous romance authors. See what books are available now and sign up to get notified about new releases here…

www.dangerouspress.com

About Midnight Dynasty

The warring Morelli and Constantine families have enough bad blood to fill an ocean, and their brand new stories will be told by your favorite dangerous romance authors.

Meet the oldest Morelli brother in his own star-crossed story...

I've known all my life that the Constantines deserved to be wiped from the face of the earth, only a smoking crater left where their mansion once stood. That's my plan until I see her, the woman in gold with the sinful curves and the blonde curls.

In a single moment, she becomes my obsession...

Elaine Constantine will be mine. And her destruction is only my beginning.

My will to dominate her runs as deep as the

hate I have for her last name. No matter how beautifully she bends beneath my hands, I'll leave her shattered, a broken toy for her cruel family.

Winston Constantine is the head of the Constantine family. He's used to people bowing to his will. Money can buy anything. And anyone. Including Ash Elliot, his new maid.

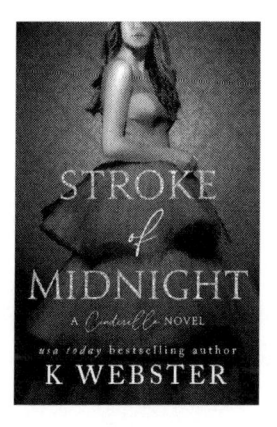

But love can have deadly consequences when it comes from a Constantine. At the stroke of midnight, that choice may be lost for both of them.

"Brilliant storytelling packed with a powerful emotional punch, it's been years since I've been so invested in a book. Erotic romance at its finest!"

– #1 New York Times bestselling author Rachel Van Dyken

"Stroke of Midnight is by far the hottest book I've read in a very long time! Winston Constantine is a dirty talking alpha who makes no apologies for going after what he wants."

— USA Today bestselling author
Jenika Snow

Ready for more bad boys, more drama, and more heat? The Constantines have a resident fixer. The man they call when they need someone persuaded in a violent fashion. Ronan was danger and beauty, murder and mercy.

Outside a glittering party, I saw a man in the dark. I didn't know then that he was an assassin. A hit man. A mercenary. Ronan radiated danger and beauty. Mercy and mystery.

I wanted him, but I was already promised to another man. Ronan might be the one who murdered him. But two warring families want my blood. I don't know where to turn.

In a mad world of luxury and secrets, he's the only one I can trust.

"M. O'Keefe brings her A-game in this sexy, complicated romance where you're left questioning if everything you thought was true while dying to get your hands on the next book!"

– New York Times bestselling author
K. Bromberg

SIGN UP FOR THE NEWSLETTER
www.dangerouspress.com

JOIN THE FACEBOOK GROUP HERE
www.dangerouspress.com/facebook

FOLLOW US ON INSTAGRAM
www.instagram.com/dangerouspress

About Skye Warren

Skye Warren is the New York Times bestselling author of dangerous romance such as the Endgame trilogy. Her books have been featured in Jezebel, Buzzfeed, USA Today Happily Ever After, Glamour, and Elle Magazine. She makes her home in Texas with her loving family, sweet dogs, and evil cat.

Sign up for Skye's newsletter:
www.skyewarren.com/newsletter

Like Skye Warren on Facebook:
facebook.com/skyewarren

Join Skye Warren's Dark Room reader group:
skyewarren.com/darkroom

Follow Skye Warren on Instagram:
instagram.com/skyewarrenbooks

Visit Skye's website for her current booklist:
www.skyewarren.com

Copyright

This is a work of fiction. Any resemblance to actual persons, living or dead, business establishments, events or locales is entirely coincidental. All rights reserved. Except for use in a review, the reproduction or use of this work in any part is forbidden without the express written permission of the author.

ONE FOR THE MONEY © 2022 by Skye Warren
Print Edition

Cover design: Damonza